Stacey and the Fashion Victim

Other books by
Ann M. Martin

Leo the Magnificat
Rachel Parker, Kindergarten Show-off
Eleven Kids, One Summer
Ma and Pa Dracula
Yours Turly, Shirley
Ten Kids, No Pets
Slam Book
Just a Summer Romance
Missing Since Monday
With You and Without You
Me and Katie (the Pest)
Stage Fright
Inside Out
Bummer Summer

THE KIDS IN MS. COLMAN'S CLASS series
BABY-SITTERS LITTLE SISTER series
THE BABY-SITTERS CLUB mysteries
THE BABY-SITTERS CLUB series

Stacey and the Fashion Victim

Ann M. Martin

AN
APPLE
PAPERBACK

SCHOLASTIC INC.
New York Toronto London Auckland Sydney

Cover art by Hodges Soileau

No part of this publication may be reproduced in whole or in part, or stored in a retrieval system, or transmitted in any form or by any means, electronic, mechanical, photocopying, recording, or otherwise, without written permission of the publisher. For information regarding permission, write to Scholastic Inc., 555 Broadway, New York, NY 10012.

ISBN 0-590-69177-5

12 11 10 9 8 7 6 5 4 3 2 1   7 8 9/9 0 1 2/0

Printed in the U.S.A.   40

First Scholastic printing, April 1997

The author gratefully acknowledges
Ellen Miles
for her help in
preparing this manuscript.

CHAPTER 1

"We're here talking to Ms. Stacey McGill, the most powerful young woman in fashion today." I was standing in front of my full-length mirror, holding my hairbrush as if it were a microphone and speaking in a deep announcer's voice. "Tell us, Ms. McGill, how did it all begin? You're only eighteen, yet you command the entire New York fashion industry."

I put the hairbrush into my other hand, turned so that I was facing in the other direction, and pretended to answer the interviewer's question, using a more grown-up, sophisticated version of my own voice. "Well, Bob, it all started back when I was thirteen and in eighth grade. I was living in the quaint little town of Stoneybrook, Connecticut, at the time. Have you heard of it?" I tossed my hair back and smiled. Of course Bob had heard of it. Now that I was so famous, everyone had heard of Stoneybrook.

1

I switched the hairbrush again. "That's where you spent your teen years, isn't it?" I asked in Bob's voice.

"That's right," I answered, switching hairbrush and voice once more. "And I'll never forget the wonderful friends I had — "

"Stacey!" That was my mother's voice, and she sounded cross. She was calling me from downstairs.

Oops. Back to Reality Land. I put down the hairbrush and ran to the door. "What?" I yelled.

"That's the fourth time I've called you," she yelled back. "We need to leave in fifteen minutes, and you haven't even had breakfast yet. Let's move it, okay?"

"Be right down!" I said. It was time to hustle. The interview was over, and so was my fantasy. Instead of the most powerful woman in fashion, I was a thirteen-year-old middle school student. Oh, well. It had been fun to dream. And I knew my mom wouldn't be too mad if she knew what I'd been up to. After all, that's what today was all about: career dreams and how you really can make them come true.

It was Take Our Daughters to Work Day, the day every April when parents all across the country bring their young daughters to work with them so the girls see that they can be anything they want to be. The day lets girls find

2

out what certain jobs are really like, and try them on for size. All of my friends — the ones I had started to tell "Bob" about — would be taking part. I was psyched about going to work with my mom, who is a buyer at Stoneybrook's biggest (actually, Stoneybrook's *only*) department store: Bellair's.

I've loved fashion for as long as I can remember. When I was in kindergarten and the other kids were drawing houses and dogs, I was drawing dresses and shoes. In first grade, I passed over *Highlights* and looked at my mother's *Vogue* magazines instead. By third grade, I was in charge of costumes for our school play.

I grew up in Manhattan, and I always preferred Macy's to the zoo, Bloomingdale's to the circus. Early on, I became a knowledgeable and talented shopper. I could — and still can — sniff out a bargain anywhere. I have an eye for what's trendy and what's classic. (I love both looks. Classics are great for building a wardrobe, and trendy clothes are just plain fun.)

Someday I'd like to be a designer, or maybe the editor of a fashion magazine, or even the owner of some major fashion-oriented business. (I have a head for figures. Math is my best subject.) But I hope I'll always have a life, too. I mean, I like other things besides fashion. For

3

example, I love kids, which is why I'm a member of the BSC, or Baby-sitters Club (more about that later). And I never want to be a workaholic like my dad. He just doesn't know when to quit, which is a big part of the reason that he and my mom are divorced. (He still lives in Manhattan, and I visit him as often as I can.)

Anyway, as you can imagine, I was looking forward to my day at Bellair's. My mom and I have been very close, especially since the divorce. I'm an only child, so it's just the two of us now. I actually like spending time with my mom, which I know is fairly unusual for a thirteen-year-old. (That's not to say that she doesn't embarrass me occasionally, or that we never fight.) And, while I have a pretty good idea of what my mom does at work, I've never spent a big block of time watching her in action. And today I was not only going to watch, but I'd be helping out. I had a feeling it was going to be an interesting day.

I checked myself one more time in the mirror. I'd dressed extra carefully, in a white linen blouse, a navy skirt, and heels. I wanted to look mature and a little sophisticated, so I'd skipped the fun hair accessories I sometimes wear to school, and put my curly (permed) blonde hair up in a simple twist. A dab of pink lip gloss, a quick sweep of mascara (it brings out my blue eyes), and I was ready.

I headed downstairs and found my mom sitting at the kitchen table. She looked up at me and smiled. "You look nice, sweetie," she said. I guess she'd forgiven me for being such a slowpoke.

"Thanks," I answered. "You do, too." I rummaged around in the cereal cabinet, looking for the Grape Nuts. Then I sat down with a bowl of cereal, a glass of orange juice, and a banana. Nice, balanced breakfast, right? You bet. Sometimes I'd just like to grab a doughnut, or even skip breakfast altogether, the way some of my friends do. But I can't. I have diabetes, which means that my body doesn't process sugars and carbohydrates correctly. If I don't watch what I eat, I can become extremely sick.

I also have to check my blood sugar regularly. I'd already done so that morning, up in my room. I have to prick my finger for a drop of blood, put it on a test strip, and check the reading my little electronic monitor gives me. The number I see there tells me how I'm doing and helps me determine how much insulin I need to take. Insulin is a hormone that my body doesn't produce the way it should, so I have to give myself shots of it every day. Sounds gross, I know. I don't like it, but I don't have any choice in the matter, so I try to make the best of it.

Just as I wolfed down the last bite of cereal, my mom glanced at her watch. "Whoa!" she said. "Time to go." She threw back her last gulp of coffee while I put my bowl in the sink. Then she grabbed her pocketbook, and I grabbed my mini-backpack, and we flew out the door.

We kept on flying all day. I never knew how busy my mom is at work, or how many responsibilities she has. It's awesome! She has an office, but she barely has the chance to sit down in it. She spends her whole day running around the store — checking on what's selling, making decisions about which items should be reduced in price in order to make room for newer things, and keeping up with the latest fashion news. Plus, she's responsible for seeing representatives, or reps, from clothing companies. They're the people who sell clothes to stores. They work two seasons ahead (which means Mom's looking at fall things now), so she has to decide, on the spot, what will sell and what won't — six months into the future!

Needless to say, it's a high-pressure job. And she loves it.

Mom motored through the day, making huge decisions left and right and plowing through mountains of work as if they were nothing. My mother is one cool woman. If I'm anywhere nearly as successful in my future career, I'll be happy.

My favorite part of the day was when we met with some sportswear reps. They'd brought piles of clothing for fall — gorgeous sweaters, jackets, and pants in colors and fabrics that made me look forward to September. Just seeing a brown tweed skirt can make me think of crisp fall days and new notebooks and the smell of burning leaves.

"Do you like this jacket, Stacey?" my mom asked, holding out a blazer in a smoky blue knit.

"It's gorgeous," I said softly, touching the fabric.

"What about these?" she asked, pointing to the square white buttons marching down the front of the jacket. She looked doubtful.

"They're a little silly," I mused. "They look like Chiclets. Something more elegant — maybe gold? — would look a lot better."

My mom turned to the sales rep, and within a few minutes she'd received a promise that the jacket could be delivered with gold buttons. "You made the call," she said, giving me a little hug. "Because of you, everyone in Stoneybrook will be wearing gold buttons this fall."

"Cool!" I said.

Just then, one of my mother's coworkers stopped by. Her name was Mrs. Maslin. Mom had introduced us earlier that day. She'd only been working at Bellair's for a couple of months, which is why I hadn't met her before. She was a short, round woman with curly brown hair and a cheerful smile. She seemed like a real dynamo. Every time we'd run into her she had either been talking into a cellular phone as she walked around, writing on the clipboard she carried everywhere, or giving hurried instructions to her secretary, who was following her around with another clipboard. (A little girl trailed after her, too. I figured she must be her daughter.)

Another thing I noticed each time we ran into her was the way she looked at me. She seemed to take me in from head to foot, with one quick glance. She did it again as she came into the room where Mom and I had just finished looking at sportswear.

"Stacey," she said, "let me ask you something. Have you ever considered modeling? If not, you should, because you have real potential. You carry yourself well, you have good bones, and you clearly have a sense of style."

Mrs. Maslin was a fast talker. I could barely fit a word in. When she stopped for breath, I told her a little about the time I entered a modeling contest at Bellair's. I won, but it wasn't a great experience. In fact, it was something I'd rather have forgotten about.

"What a pity," she said, shaking her head. "I'd like you to have a positive modeling experience. Have you heard about Fashion Week?"

Before I could even nod or shake my head, she was off and running.

"Fashion Week is an annual event here at Bellair's, and I'm in charge of making this year's the best ever. Not only will we be hosting small fashion shows every day next week — with a huge one at the end of the week — but Bellair's will be the site of the photo shoot for this year's national catalog. We've hired most of our professional models already, but headquarters has told me they also want some fresh new faces for the catalog, and I think you'd be perfect. The pay, by the way, is excellent."

"Well," I began. I couldn't help feeling excited about the idea, and I was flattered by Mrs. Maslin's high opinion of my looks. Still, I wasn't crazy about the idea of modeling again. And I noticed, out of the corner of my eye, that my mother was shaking her head.

"I don't know," she said. "Stacey's only thirteen — "

"It's just for a few days. She'll have a wonderful time!" exclaimed Mrs. Maslin. "And don't worry, I'll take good care of her."

"What about school?" asked my mom.

"All the events take place after school hours," said Mrs. Maslin. "We don't want to disrupt the academic schedules of any of our girls."

"I could put the money in my college fund," I said to my mom. Suddenly, I wanted to take part in Fashion Week. It'd be fun to hang around with real models and to wear all the latest styles. I crossed my fingers and smiled hopefully at my mother.

Mrs. Maslin knew enough to stay quiet for a moment and give my mom a chance to make up her mind.

Finally, Mom smiled. "Well, I suppose it's all right," she said. "But only if Stacey can quit if she feels at all uncomfortable, or if her school-work suffers."

"Of course," agreed Mrs. Maslin. She smiled at me. "Orientation is this Saturday."

"Yyyyesss!" I said. "Thanks, Mom," I remembered to add.

Stacey McGill, Supermodel. My career in fashion was starting even sooner than I'd dreamed.

CHAPTER 2

"I swear, I didn't understand a word anyone said all day!" Claudia Kishi helped herself to a handful of Skittles. "Other than 'lunchtime,' that is." She giggled. "I guess I'll never be an investment manager. Big surprise, right?"

We all cracked up. Imagining Claudia as an investment manager was nearly impossible. She's my best friend, and I love her dearly, but saying that she doesn't care much about numbers is the understatement of the year. She'd make such a mess of everyone's investments that the world economy would probably explode or something.

It was later that afternoon, and I was sitting in Claudia's bedroom along with the rest of the members of the BSC. Between phone calls, we were talking about the experiences we'd had during Take Our Daughters to Work Day. The BSC meets in Claud's room on Mondays, Wednesdays, and Fridays from five-thirty until six, and parents call us during those times to set up baby-sitting jobs. We're more like a baby-sitting business than a club — a business that works very, very well. We're super-organized. We maintain a club record book with up-to-date information on our clients, and a calendar with our schedules. We also keep a club notebook, in which we each write up every single one of our jobs. That way we all stay aware of what's going on with the kids we sit for. The parents love that.

We're excellent sitters, if I do say so myself. Every BSC member is responsible, punctual, and caring. It's easy when you love kids the way we do. We love hanging out with them, playing with them, *doing* things with them. We're not the kind of sitters who plop the kids in front of the TV and spend the whole time raiding the fridge and talking on the phone. We'd rather unpack our Kid-Kits (boxes we've filled with fun stuff such as stickers and markers and hand-me-down toys and books) and have a good time with our charges. Our charges love us. Which is why the parents keep hiring us. Which is why the BSC is so successful.

"I didn't understand much about what my mom was doing, either," said Kristy Thomas, who's president of the BSC. "But I reorganized her desk so she'll be able to work much more efficiently."

Everybody cracked up again. It wasn't hard to picture Kristy taking charge of her mother's office. Kristy's just a take-charge person. And she's always coming up with excellent ideas. For example, all the things I just told you about the BSC — the club itself, how it works, the club record book, the Kid-Kits — were Kristy's ideas. That's why she's president.

Kristy is on the short side and has brown hair and eyes. She's about as interested in fashion as Claudia is in investments. In fact, I've rarely seen her wearing anything but her "uniform," which consists of jeans, running shoes, and a turtleneck — or a T-shirt, if it's summer.

Make that a "Krushers" T-shirt. As if her life weren't busy enough, Kristy coaches a softball team (called Kristy's Krushers) she formed for little kids. That's the kind of person Kristy is.

I think she inherited a lot of her determination and strength from her mom, who brought up four kids (Kristy and her three brothers — Charlie and Sam, who are older, and David Michael, who is younger) on her own after Mr. Thomas walked out on the family, years ago. Kristy's mom definitely deserved a break, and she got one when she met Watson Brewer, a truly nice guy, a millionaire, and now Kristy's stepfather. Watson has two kids of his own from his first marriage — a boy named Andrew and a girl named Karen. When he and Kristy's mom married, they decided to adopt one more child together, and that's how Emily Michelle, the world's cutest toddler, came to live with Kristy's family. Now Kristy's grandmother Nannie lives with them, too, and so does an assortment of pets. Fortunately, Watson's mansion is huge. And well organized, thanks to Kristy.

"Anybody want some more Skittles?" Claudia asked, passing the bag around. She's vice-president of the BSC. We meet in her room because she's the only one of us who has her own phone, which means we don't have to worry about tying up anyone's family line. As VP, Claudia doesn't have any official duties, but she's made it her *unofficial* duty to supply munchies for our meetings.

Supplying food is no hardship for Claudia. Junk food is one of her great loves, and seeing her friends chewing away on Ring-Dings and pretzels makes her happy. Her parents aren't crazy about Claudia's junk food habit, and they don't like her reading habits, either. (Claudia's a Nancy Drew fanatic, and her mom, a librarian, doesn't approve.) That's why a careful search of Claudia's room will always reveal secret stashes of candy bars and mysteries.

Claudia's older sister, Janine, is a certified genius. She and Claudia are like night and day, especially when it comes to school. In fact, Claudia has had so much trouble in school that she is now repeating seventh grade. And she's doing well there. She's not dumb; it's just that she isn't interested in the things Janine loves, such as math and science. On the other hand, I doubt Janine knows the difference between acrylics and oil paints, and she probably couldn't sculpt with papier-mâché if her life depended on it. Claudia, however, is the most talented artist I know. Recently, she won first prize in an art show, and she was by far the youngest person to enter it. We were so, so proud of her.

Claudia's artistic nature doesn't stop at putting colors on paper, though. She sees everything as a blank canvas: her room, her body, her face. She has the funkiest, wildest style. No outfit is too over-the-top, no hairstyle too extreme. We're great shopping buddies, she and I.

Claudia passed the Skittles to Mary Anne Spier, who was happy to take some. "Well, I had fun today," she said as she shook a few out of the bag. "But I don't know if I'd ever want to be a lawyer. They have to be so mean sometimes. Think of all those courtroom movies with a lawyer making the witness cry. Forget it. I could never do that."

"But your dad's not a prosecutor, is he?" I asked. It was just like Mary Anne to worry about having to be mean.

She shook her head. "No, he does corporate law," she admitted. "He's hardly ever in court. He was just working on a case today. And he let me look stuff up for him."

Mary Anne is Kristy's best friend, even though you'd never expect them to be buds. Mary Anne is as shy and sweet as Kristy is bold and brash. They look alike, though. Mary Anne has brown eyes and hair (cut in a slightly trendier style) and is also on the short side.

Mary Anne is the club's secretary, which means she keeps track of our schedules and job bookings. She's excellent at it and never makes mistakes.

She's close to her dad, since she grew up with him as her only parent. (Her mom died when Mary Anne was just a baby.) These days, Mary Anne has a stepmother, Sharon Schafer, who happens to be the mother of Mary Anne's other best friend, Dawn. Mary Anne and Dawn met when Dawn and her younger brother, Jeff, moved here from California, after their mom and dad divorced. (Sharon had grown up in Stoneybrook, so it made sense for her to come back home.) Soon after they became friends, Mary Anne and Dawn discovered that Sharon and Mary Anne's dad, Richard, used to date back in high school. Before long, Dawn and Mary Anne were best friends *and* stepsisters.

By that time, Jeff had decided that he'd never fit in on the East Coast, and he'd gone back to California to live with his dad. Dawn visited them often, until she finally realized that her heart belonged out there, too. Now she's a full-time Californian, though she visits Stoneybrook on school vacations and in the summer. I know Mary Anne misses her a ton between visits. We all do.

Fortunately, Mary Anne has her kitten, Tigger, and her boyfriend, Logan Bruno, to comfort her. Logan's a great guy and very cute, too. Not only that, he's an excellent baby-sitter and happens to be an associate member of the BSC. He and our other associate member, Shannon Kilbourne, don't have to come to meetings, but they're on standby if we need extra sitters. Shannon, who lives in Kristy's neighborhood, goes to private school and is one of those terrific students who participates in a million clubs and still manages to pull great grades.

Are you wondering about my job in the club? Well, I'm the treasurer. I collect dues every Monday (my fellow members love to give me a hard time about separating them from their hard-earned dollars) and keep track of how much we have in the treasury. Then, when we need money to help pay Claudia's phone bill or Kristy's transportation costs (her brother Charlie drives her to meetings, so we chip in for his gas), I hand it out. My friends are amazed at how I can keep track of every cent, but I think it's easy. As I said, math comes naturally to me.

Lately, Charlie and Kristy have had another passenger, Abby Stevenson, the newest member of the BSC. She and her twin sister, Anna, and their mom moved to Kristy's neighborhood recently from Long Island. Mrs. Stevenson is an executive editor at a publishing house in Manhattan — that's where Abby had spent *her* day. Abby's and Anna's dad died several years ago in a car accident. Abby doesn't talk about him much. She'd rather make a joke, or do an impression of one of our teachers. Abby loves to make people laugh.

We invited both twins to join the club, but Anna is way too busy with her music to have time for baby-sitting. She plays violin, and I think she may want to do that professionally someday. She takes private lessons, practices constantly, and plays in the SMS orchestra. Her music is awesome.

Both twins have dark eyes and thick, dark, curly hair. Anna's is shorter, and Abby's is longer. They both wear contacts, or glasses, depending on what they're doing. Abby wears contacts when she's playing soccer or softball or running in a track meet; she's a natural athlete. She also has a million allergies, plus asthma, but she doesn't let that slow her down.

Abby took over Dawn's role in the club, which means she's the alternate officer. If one of the other officers can't make it to a meeting, Abby does that person's job.

" — so then I convinced Sherry — she's my mom's assistant — to let me do the copying. Because I wanted to try copying my face. There I was, with my forehead pressed against the glass, when who walks in but my mom's boss! Fortunately, she has a sense of humor." Abby was laughing as she told the story of her day, and we were all laughing with her.

"I did the same thing at *my* mom's office!" said Jessi, giggling. "It's a good thing I didn't get caught. My mom's boss doesn't have a sense of humor at all."

Jessi Ramsey is one of the club's two junior officers. Unlike the rest of us, who are thirteen, Jessi and her best friend, Mallory Pike, are eleven. Being junior officers means that at night, they can only sit for their own families, so they take a lot of our afternoon jobs.

Jessi's mom is in advertising, and Mal's works as a temporary secretary, so both of them had plenty of office stories for us. "Personally, I think I'd rather work as a horse trainer or something," said Mal. "That is, if I couldn't be a writer." She and Jessi are both big readers who adore horse stories, and Mal would love to be a writer someday.

Jessi is African-American, with cocoa-colored skin, dark eyes, and the long, muscular limbs of a trained dancer. (She's a serious ballet student and practices all the time.) She has a younger sister named Becca and a baby brother nicknamed Squirt. Their aunt Cecelia lives with the family, too.

Mal, who has curly reddish-brown hair, glasses, and braces, has a much larger family. There are eight Pike kids in all. Mal, as the oldest, has had plenty of baby-sitting practice. I bet she'll grow up to write funny stories about her huge family.

Guess what. Mal — and a couple of my other friends — weren't thrilled to hear about the offer Mrs. Maslin had made me.

"I hate all this model stuff," Mal complained. "Why should people be paid millions of dollars just because they happen to have good genes? I'd like to see girls admiring women scientists or senators, instead of looking up to models. What's so great about somebody who can prance around looking good in clothes? Life is not a beauty contest."

Jessi was nodding, and so was Kristy. But Mary Anne was, as always, ready to see both sides. "Fashion Week isn't a beauty contest," she reminded Mal gently. "And modeling can be a good way for a woman to become independent."

"And be too busy to do her job," Kristy grumbled. "How are we supposed to cover all our baby-sitting work without you?"

"It's only a few days," I said. "And we haven't been too busy lately. I promise to take extra jobs the week after, to make up for any I miss." I paused, hoping Kristy wouldn't mind what I had to say next. "By the way," I added carefully. "If we're still not too busy during Fashion Week, there may be some work at Bellair's. I know the Kid Center will probably need extra help." Bellair's has this great in-store day-care center. I'd worked there before, and I knew they appreciated experienced help.

I was hoping some of my friends would be around to enjoy Fashion Week with me. I had a feeling it was going to be a blast, and I knew it would be even more fun if some of my BSC friends were on hand.

CHAPTER 3

"Pssst! Stacey! Over here!"

I looked, gasped, and looked again. "Oh, no," I murmured. "Of all people." I glanced behind me, almost hoping that Mary Anne or Mal or Claudia might still be there, but they'd all gone their separate ways. I was on my own.

With Cokie Mason.

It was orientation day for Fashion Week, and I was just arriving for the models' meeting. Mary Anne and Mal had headed off for their meeting — they'd signed up to work in the Kid Center — and Claudia was here to see the staff that had come to shoot the catalog. My mom and Mrs. Maslin had arranged for her to work as an intern with the art director for the shoot, and Claudia was thrilled.

So I was on my own as I entered the large meeting room. I'd been nervous about that. I knew the room would be packed with utterly gorgeous girls, and I hated having to walk in there by myself. I was wishing for a friendly face to greet me.

Be careful of what you wish for. It may come true. (My mother has said that to me, but I never really knew what she meant by that. Until now.)

Cokie's face was friendly, all right, as she waved me over to an empty seat next to hers. But it was a superficial kind of friendly. You know how some people smile with their whole face and some people smile with just their lips? Well, Cokie's mouth was smiling, but that was it.

Cokie Mason is not exactly a friend, though she does attend my school, Stoneybrook Middle School, and I've known her for awhile. The problem with Cokie is that she always feels this need to be better, to compete, to win. And in her mind the biggest contest is the one for popularity. I guess I should feel sorry for her, but it's tough to, after some of the tricks she's pulled. Believe it or not, she once even tried to steal Logan from Mary Anne.

Anyway, there she was, the only person I knew in the room. And next to her was that empty seat. What could I do? I sat down next to her. She was wearing designer jeans and a designer T-shirt, and on her lap was a designer backpack. Cokie has no personal sense of style. She thinks that if an item of clothing costs a lot and has some famous person's name on it, it must be cool.

Do I sound catty?

I don't mean to. I guess Cokie's attitude is catching. She is the biggest gossip and loves nothing better than putting people down behind their backs.

I must admit that, as much as her huge appetite for gossip bugs me, it did come in handy that day. Cokie had made it her priority to find out everything there was to know about the important people in that room, and by the end of the meeting she'd made sure to fill me in. I knew better than to take everything she told me as the truth. Still, it was a good way to begin to sort out who was who.

I almost missed her rundown, though, because I started out our conversation by insulting her — accidentally. "What are *you* doing here?" I asked. I was simply surprised to see her.

"What's that supposed to mean? That I'm not pretty enough to be a model?" Cokie said, glaring.

"No — I — that's not what I meant!" I exclaimed, blushing.

"Well, for your information, I was spotted by an agent. Dylan Trueheart. I'm sure you've heard of him, since he's one of the top agents in modeling."

I'd never heard the name in my life, but I

didn't want to insult Cokie any further, so I just nodded.

"He saw me one day last week while I was shopping in the Juniors department. He discovered me, just like that!" Cokie was glowing. I had a feeling that being "discovered" by Dylan Trueheart was the high point of her life so far.

"Cool," I said.

Just then, Mrs. Maslin stood up in front of the room. "Girls!" she called out loudly. I could barely hear her voice over the buzz of voices in the room. "May I have your attention, please?"

The noise began to fade, and finally all eyes were turned toward Mrs. Maslin. "Welcome," she said. "I want to congratulate you on being chosen to participate in Fashion Week at Bellair's."

"Big whoop," I heard the blonde girl next to me mutter under her breath. She looked totally bored as she sipped from a bottle of water.

Mrs. Maslin, fortunately, didn't seem to hear her. She went on, telling us about the events that would take place over the following days, starting with an informal sportswear show the next day, moving on through a series of other small fashion shows and the ongoing shoot for the catalog, and "culminating," Mrs. Maslin breathlessly told us, "in the biggest fashion show this area has ever seen."

The girl next to me was rolling her eyes.

Mrs. Maslin described the final show, telling us about the music, the lights, the excitement. "And for the finale," she finished, "one of you lucky girls will come out as Princess Bellair — crown and all."

I saw Cokie's eyes light up and knew that she already wanted more than anything to be Princess Bellair.

Mrs. Maslin finished by telling us that the schedules she was handing out were "to be strictly adhered to," and that she hoped we would have "the time of our lives."

I heard the girl next to me give a little snort.

Then Mrs. Maslin introduced Mr. Bellair, the owner of the store. I've met him before, when I was visiting my mom at work. He seems like a nice enough man. He has a red face and wavy blond hair that almost looks as if he has it permed. Some men do that, according to my mom. He made a speech about how glad he was to see the "women of tomorrow" representing his store, blah, blah, blah. He went on and on, and eventually he lost his audience. Even Mrs. Maslin was ignoring him. She was flipping through her clipboard, making notes and lists. Girls were whispering and giggling as they checked their schedules and compared assignments. At first I tried to ignore them, but finally Cokie and I started whispering, too.

"See that girl next to you?" Cokie hissed. I nodded. "You know who that is, don't you?" I shook my head. "That's Sydney," Cokie said.

"Sydney who?" I whispered back, after checking to make sure the blonde girl wasn't looking our way.

"Just Sydney," said Cokie. "She's *huge*."

I glanced at the blonde girl again. "She looks teeny to me," I said.

"I mean in terms of her career," Cokie whispered, exasperated. "Didn't you see her on the cover of *Teenage Miss* last month? And she's in the new campaign for Jinky Jeans. She's only fifteen, but she's practically a supermodel. She knows it, too. She acts all stuck-up. And you know what? She used to date Roger Bellair — Mr. Bellair's son, who's going to inherit the whole Bellair's chain. He's working as a photo assistant on the shoot this week. Maybe we'll see some fireworks!"

Next, Cokie pointed to a girl with huge green eyes and straight brown hair cut in a perfect bob. "That's Harmony Skye," she whispered. "She's fourteen, and she's on her way up."

"Who's that next to her?" I asked. The woman next to Harmony was reaching over to fuss with Harmony's bangs.

"That's her mother," said Cokie. "Talk about pushy. I already saw her sucking up to Mrs.

Maslin. That woman won't rest until her daughter's face is plastered on every magazine cover in the country."

"How about that red-haired girl?" I asked. I didn't love Cokie's attitude, but I had to admit it was fun hearing about everyone.

"Cynthia Rowlands," Cokie reported. "She's sixteen. Over the hill." Cokie snickered. "Just kidding. But she *is* past her peak. Last year she was almost as big as Sydney. Now I hear she's thinking about quitting and going back to being a regular high school kid."

There were plenty of other pretty girls in the room, but only one more I was curious about. "That girl with the blonde ringlets," I said. "She looks familiar."

"That's because she's from Stoneybrook," said Cokie. "Her name's Blaine Gilbert, and she goes to boarding school in Pennsylvania when she's not busy working on her career. She's just starting out. All she's done so far is catalog work, but she's trying to make it into the big time. She was invited to be in Fashion Week when she went to Take Our Daughters to Work Day with her mom. Mrs. Gilbert works in the national office of Bellair's."

"By the way, Cokie," I said, "how did you become interested in modeling?"

"Why wouldn't I be interested?" she said.

"You make great money, meet all kinds of people, get famous — it's cool."

I had to admit she was right. If anyone was well suited for the life of a model, it was probably Cokie.

I was so busy listening to her gossip, I'd barely noticed when Mr. Bellair had finished his remarks and Mrs. Maslin had returned to the front of the room. She thanked Mr. Bellair, reminded us to be on time the next day, and said we were free to go.

Everyone stood and stretched, and then we began to file out of the room. I took one more look around, trying to remember everything Cokie had told me about the other models. The funny thing was, the girls in that room weren't what I had expected. Oh, they were pretty, all right. But they also looked ordinary, like girls I knew in school. They wore the same kinds of clothes, carried the same backpacks, had the same haircuts. They weren't really all that different from me. I could even imagine becoming friends with some of them.

I was starting to think that modeling was going to be fun this time.

CHAPTER 4

"Places, everyone, places!"

Some major hurrying and scurrying was going on in the huge, open dressing room as we — the models — rushed around trying to figure out what our "places" were supposed to be. I'd read the detailed notes Mrs. Maslin had handed out at our morning meeting, so I knew I was wearing three different outfits in this first show. I would start off wearing a raspberry-colored romper, which I was supposed to accessorize with white sneakers and a white baseball cap. (I was already dressed in the romper, but I hadn't found the hat yet.) Then I'd change into a red-and-white-striped bathing suit with a matching cover-up (plus accessories, including red thongs and a big straw hat). Finally, I'd appear in a denim minidress. With that outfit I'd wear espadrilles and an armful of colorful bangles.

Of course, my hairstyle would also change

with each outfit, from pigtails to a slicked-back look to a French braid. And each change would have to happen in under seven minutes.

Multiply that by a roomful of girls and what do you have?

Chaos, total chaos. And that was only the rehearsal.

It was Sunday, and I'd appeared at Bellair's early (following Mrs. Maslin's orders) for the sportswear show. We were going to have a quick rehearsal, then put on the show in the afternoon. This was supposed to be an informal presentation, for an invited audience of "preferred customers." At our meeting, Mrs. Maslin had told us to "think *fun*."

As if.

Fun was the last thing on my mind as I raced around trying to track down a pair of sneakers in my size, while a hairdresser raced after me trying to match hair ribbons to my romper.

Meanwhile, the other girls were racing around, too. Three were at the hairdressing station, and several others were struggling into their clothes by the big mirror. I saw a couple of girls arguing over shoes. Harmony Skye's mother was pestering Mrs. Maslin about how Harmony couldn't *possibly* appear in "that hideous excuse for a bathing suit." Cynthia Rowlands was asking everyone if they'd seen her lucky lipstick brush. Cokie was touching up her makeup for the fourth time. Blaine Gilbert couldn't make the zipper on her sundress close. And Sydney?

Sydney was completely dressed and made up. Her hair was finished. She sat calmly in a chair near the spot where we'd eventually line up to go onstage, ignoring the confusion and taking sips out of a bottle of that French water. She appeared to be above it all.

Sydney was definitely a pro.

She seemed to have a way of holding herself away from everyone else. And, while I didn't exactly *like* her, I did admire her. Why? Well, mostly because of the things she *didn't* do.

She didn't gossip about the other girls.

She didn't behave as if any food other than diet soda was the enemy.

She didn't smoke cigarettes and leave nasty butts all over the place.

And she didn't act competitive every time a good assignment was up for grabs.

These things may not seem like anything out of the ordinary, but believe me, in that group they were. I couldn't believe the way most of the models behaved. I was surprised — and a little disgusted. Make that a *lot* disgusted, when it came to the smoking. I was amazed at how many of the girls smoked. Every time there was a five-minute break, they'd rush out of the room, light up, and puff away like crazy. It was gross.

As for the gossip, that was pretty gross, too. As I've already said, I'm not crazy about dissing people behind their backs. Among this crowd, gossip was practically a world-class sport. These girls could have entered the Olympics of gossip. As soon as one girl had walked away, the others would start to dish the dirt about her. I wondered what they were saying about me, and I tried not to care.

As far as healthy eating? Well, let's put it this way. I think Sydney and I were the only girls in the group who ever ate *anything* healthy. The others seemed to think they could live on cigarettes and diet soda. When I pulled out an apple that morning, I saw a few girls looking at it as if it were radioactive.

And the competitive thing? I could have done without that, too. It was as if each of the girls felt that she had to elbow the others aside in order to make herself look good. It made for what Dawn would have called "a bad vibe." I saw girls smiling charmingly at Mrs. Maslin one second, hoping to get on her good side, then making faces at her behind her back when she gave a good assignment to somebody else.

For example, that morning everyone was whispering about how Mrs. Maslin had given

Harmony all the best clothes to model. I couldn't see what was so much better about the clothes she was wearing, but the other, more experienced models seemed to know right away which outfits carried the most prestige.

"What did she do to deserve special treatment?" I heard Cynthia Rowlands hiss.

"It's that mother of hers," whispered another girl. "Mrs. My-Daughter's-Better-Than-Everyone-Else." She made a face.

"No, it's the way Miss Harmony sucks up to old Maslin," said Cokie. "Look at her, pretending she actually likes that bratty daughter of hers." She pointed toward a corner of the dressing room, where Harmony was sitting with a little girl.

The girl was Emily Maslin, Mrs. Maslin's ten-year-old daughter, the one I'd seen trailing her on Take Our Daughters to Work Day. Mrs. Maslin had introduced us when I first arrived, but I'd barely had a chance to talk to her. From the little I'd seen, she seemed like a smart kid. She also seemed to be enthralled by the models and by the fashion scene. But I had a distinct feeling her mother wanted to discourage those feelings.

Emily had been walking around all morning, watching closely as we dressed, had our hair done, and were made up. Most of the girls treated her like a pest, but I'd noticed that Harmony was always willing to answer her questions or let her try on a blouse or a hair accessory. I could tell that Harmony actually liked Emily, but I could also see how the other girls might think she was just trying to impress Mrs. Maslin.

"Emily!" called Mrs. Maslin just then. "Leave Harmony alone. We're almost ready to start our rehearsal, and she needs to finish dressing."

"I want to be in the show, too," Emily said, pouting a little as she joined her mother. "Why can't I?"

"We've been over this," said Mrs. Maslin. "You're too young. Now, remember, I said you could come watch today as long as you promised not to bug me. Right?"

"I guess," said Emily, looking down at her shoes. "But — "

"No buts," said Mrs. Maslin. "Now, where did Sydney go? It's just about time to start." She bustled away, checking off items on the list clipped to her clipboard.

I saw Emily watch her leave, then turn and head back toward the racks of clothing. After that, I lost sight of her, since I was too busy fixing one of my pigtails.

That's when the voice started yelling "Places!" And the music started, and the curtain opened, and the lights came on. The rehearsal was about to start.

I felt my heart thumping, just a little, as I found my place in line. I knew the small auditorium wasn't yet full of people, but it was still nerve-racking to be waiting for my turn onstage.

Mrs. Maslin appeared in front of us, just offstage, and began to give directions. "Go, Harmony," she said, giving her a hand signal. "And you're next, Cynthia. Heads up. Smile! Don't forget to turn twice at the end of the runway. And show off the lining of that jacket. Good! Okay, next! Let's go. Heads up!"

She sounded like a drill sergeant.

When my turn came, I put my chin in the air, plastered what I hoped was a gorgeous smile across my face, took three big steps — and tripped over a cable taped to the floor. Fortunately, I was still offstage when that happened.

That wasn't the only glitch in the morning's rehearsal. There were a lot of them. The music cues weren't perfect, the lighting was uneven, and a few of the girls forgot the direction in which to turn. Still, there were no major disasters, and by the end of the rehearsal I felt a lot more confident about having to "walk the walk" in front of an audience.

"That was great, Stace!" said Claudia, giving me a hug after the rehearsal.

"You saw it?" I asked. I hadn't noticed any-one watching.

"Sure, we were all out there," she answered. "The whole catalog crew. And guess who couldn't keep his eyes off a certain model?" She nodded toward the back of the room, and I saw Roger Bellair talking eagerly to Sydney. He seemed thrilled to be near her, but she wore her usual "I'm-so-incredibly-bored" ex-pression.

"Doesn't exactly look like the romance of the century," I commented.

"Girls! Girls!" Mrs. Maslin materialized in the middle of the room, clapping her hands for attention. "I want to go over a few notes with you before the show. Can everyone please gather around?"

Claudia grinned at me and waved. "I'm out of here," she said. I could tell she was glad not to be part of that chaotic scene.

I waved good-bye and settled down to hear Mrs. Maslin's notes. She'd noticed a lot of de-tails I'd missed — little things that had gone wrong during the rehearsal. She had some-thing to say to nearly every girl there. (She told me I'd walked too fast and that I needed to smile more.) Every girl but Harmony, who had apparently done a perfect job. I saw a couple of the girls shoot her nasty looks.

After that, it was time to prepare for the actual show, and there wasn't a minute to waste. Once again, the dressing room buzzed as we ran around frantically. Once again, somebody started yelling "Places." And once again, I found myself in line, waiting nervously for my first real trip down the runway.

Thanks to our rehearsal, everything went perfectly smoothly. And, despite my butterflies, I found out that it was actually fun.

There was only one hitch during the show, and I had to admit it was kind of a funny one. At a moment when her mom was distracted, Emily managed to run out onstage to "model" an outfit she'd put together all on her own.

Mrs. Maslin wasn't amused, but the audience loved Emily.

Afterward, as we relaxed in the dressing room, I was sitting by the makeup mirror talking with Cokie about how well everything had gone.

Suddenly, I heard a wild shriek.

CHAPTER 5

"Poison! My baby's been poisoned!"

It was Mrs. Skye who was shrieking as she ran toward Harmony.

Harmony, who had been sitting at her dressing table sipping a cup of tea, was slumped over, moaning as she clutched her stomach.

Cokie and I looked at each other in shock. Then we ran to see if Harmony was okay.

"Sweetie, speak to me! Are you all right?" Mrs. Skye was bent over her daughter. "Somebody call security," she yelled. "Call an ambulance!"

"I don't need an ambulance," Harmony mumbled. "Just need — just need a little nap." She rested her head on the dressing table. Her face was white and pasty.

I glanced at the cup she'd been drinking from. It was nearly empty, but what was left in it looked like ordinary tea. "Are you sure she's not just sick? What makes you think she was poisoned?" I asked her mother. I didn't mean to sound nosy, but I couldn't help wondering. She seemed so sure.

"Because Harmony never eats a thing on the day of a show," she snapped. "That tea is the first thing that's passed her lips since dinnertime last night." She tugged at her daughter's arm. "Darling! Sweetie! Please tell me you're all right."

"I'm okay, Mom," Harmony said. I could tell it was an effort for her to talk. "Stomach just hurts. Bad." She was still clutching her stomach.

A security guard had arrived by then, and so had Mrs. Maslin. "What seems to be the trouble?" asked Mrs. Maslin.

"Somebody poisoned my daughter," said Mrs. Skye. "I think she's going to be all right. But obviously the security staff here is not doing a proper job."

The man looked offended.

Mrs. Maslin jumped in. "I'm sure they're doing everything they can," she said soothingly. "I've made it clear that the safety of these girls is our highest priority." She nodded at the guard. "Thanks, Jim," she said. "You can stop in at my office later and we'll file a report."

He left, looking angry.

Mrs. Maslin turned to Mrs. Skye. "Are you absolutely sure you want to report this?" she asked quietly. "News of a poisoning might find its way into the papers."

"You're just worried about Bellair's reputation," said Mrs. Skye angrily. "What about Harmony?"

"It's Harmony I'm concerned about," said Mrs. Maslin. "Harmony's career could be affected — negatively — by something like this. Even if it wasn't her fault. And Bellair's could be affected, too. In fact, maybe it would be best for both Harmony and Bellair's if Harmony were to withdraw from Fashion Week."

"No!" Mrs. Skye cried. "I mean," Mrs. Skye narrowed her eyes, considering (I could practically see the wheels turning inside her head) "I think you may be right," she said finally. "Perhaps a formal report and investigation aren't necessary." She gave Mrs. Maslin a tight-lipped smile. "Maybe it's just a little stomach bug, after all."

"Harmony, do you want to lie down?" Mrs. Maslin asked.

Harmony shook her head. "I'm okay, really," she insisted.

"What happened?" asked Blaine Gilbert, who had pushed her way into the circle of people surrounding Harmony. By that time, nearly all the girls in the room had gathered near Harmony's dressing table.

"Let's all move back a little and give Harmony some room to breathe in," said Mrs. Maslin. "She's going to be just fine. She's just having a little stomach trouble."

"Just a little stomach trouble," repeated Mrs. Skye obediently.

"I thought I heard something about poison," said Blaine.

"Now, now," said Mrs. Maslin. "Let's not jump to conclusions. Why would anyone want to hurt Harmony?" She smiled. "We're all friends here, right?"

Nobody said anything.

Mrs. Maslin pretended not to notice. "In any case, Harmony is clearly not seriously ill. Right, dear?" she asked, touching Harmony's shoulder.

Harmony looked miserable. "Right," she answered.

"But if you're not feeling up to it, perhaps I should change the assignments around so you have less work this week."

I was nearly positive that I noticed a tiny smile on Cynthia Rowlands' lips when Mrs. Maslin said that. But I could be wrong.

Harmony hesitated. She was looking a little better already, although her face was still very white. "Well, maybe I — " She glanced at her mother. "I mean, I'd hate to miss anything, but — "

"I won't hear of it!" said Mrs. Skye. "My

Harmony *lives* for modeling, and now you want to take it away from her. How could you!"

"Mom, nobody's taking anything away — " Harmony began. She looked awfully embarrassed by the way her mother was carrying on. I noticed some of the other models snickering a little, which couldn't have helped. Harmony's face wasn't so white anymore. In fact, it was turning a deep pink as she listened to her mother's protests.

Mrs. Maslin held up her hands in an "I surrender" gesture. "Fine, fine," she said. "I never said I *wanted* Harmony to drop out of Fashion Week. In fact, I was counting on her professionalism. Harmony is a wonderful, talented model, and I'm thrilled to have her aboard."

Now Harmony was really blushing.

Behind Mrs. Maslin's back, some of the girls were making nasty faces, and one of them was silently imitating her. Neither Harmony nor her mother noticed, though. They were too busy packing up her things and preparing to leave.

"We'll be here tomorrow," said Mrs. Skye as she helped Harmony put on her backpack. "Count on it."

She made it sound like a threat.

"Good, good," said Mrs. Maslin. "We're all done for today, anyway. Now, Harmony, you take care of yourself tonight. And if you still feel bad tomorrow — "

"She'll be fine," interrupted Mrs. Skye. She put her arm around Harmony's shoulder and pushed through the crowd of girls. "No thanks to whoever is trying to put her out of the picture," she added under her breath, giving a narrow-eyed glare at the circle of models. "This business is so competitive," she murmured as she and her daughter moved off.

"Yeah, and you're one of the worst," said the girl standing next to me, whispering. "That woman is like a shark," she added, heading for her own dressing table.

"I can't believe she thought her precious was poisoned," said another girl.

"Maybe she was, though," I heard someone else say. "Or maybe the poison was meant for somebody else. I mean, that tea just came from the refreshment table, right? Anybody could have taken it."

I gulped when I heard that. It was true. How could a poisoner have known that Harmony would take that particular cup? It could easily have been grabbed by another girl. Or — I could have taken it. I could have been poisoned.

"Creepy, huh?"

I jumped. It was as if someone were reading

my thoughts. I turned to see Claudia, who was shaking her head.

"I just heard what happened," she said. "I can't believe it."

Just then, Mallory and Mary Anne poked their heads around the corner of the mirrored wall of my dressing table. "Pizza, anyone?" asked Mary Anne cheerfully.

"We've been chasing kids around all day, and we're *starving*," added Mal.

Obviously, they hadn't heard the news yet. Claudia and I exchanged glances. "Pizza sounds great," I said. "Anyway, we have to talk to you guys. We just might have a mystery on our hands."

Mal's eyes lit up. She *adores* mysteries.

Mary Anne looked worried. "What happened?" she asked.

"We'll fill you in at Pizza Express," I said. There was enough talk going on in the dressing room. I didn't want to add to it.

The four of us headed out of Bellair's and went straight to Pizza Express. We ordered a large pie, half of which was topped with pepperoni and the other half with mushrooms. When the waitress brought our sodas, we settled in to talk.

"So, what's up?" asked Mal. "Spill it, before I die of curiosity."

"Well," I said, lowering my voice. "It looks as if one of the girls was poisoned today."

"Poisoned?" Mal cried.

"Shhh!" I said. "The whole world doesn't have to know about it."

"Is she all right?" asked Mary Anne anxiously.

I nodded. "She's going to be fine," I said. "But the thing is, nobody knows who did it — or why."

"I have a few guesses," Claudia said meaningfully.

"You do?" I asked. "Who?"

"Wait a minute," said Mal. "Back up first and tell us all the details." She frowned. "I should probably be taking notes for the mystery notebook," she added.

The mystery notebook is another of Kristy's great ideas. The BSC has been involved in solving lots of mysteries. In the past, we'd write down notes about suspects and clues on whatever piece of paper was at hand. But that usually turned out to be a grocery list, or someone's English homework, which meant our notes were frequently lost. Kristy came up with the idea of keeping a notebook just for mysteries, and ever since then we've been the most organized detectives around.

"We can write it all down later," Claudia told her. "Go on, Stace."

Just then our pizza arrived, so we paused for a moment as we each took a slice. I suddenly realized that I was very, very hungry.

After I'd taken a few bites, I began to tell Mal and Mary Anne what had happened.

"So you really think it was poison?" asked Mal, wide-eyed.

"Mrs. Skye seemed pretty sure of it," I said. "At least, she did at first."

"But that's awful!" said Mary Anne. "I mean, it could have been anyone. It could have been you!" She looked terrified.

"I know," I said. "I thought of the same thing. But it's okay. Harmony's going to be fine." I had to reassure Mary Anne, or she'd probably worry about me all week. I turned to Claudia. "So who is your suspect?" I asked.

"It's obvious," she said. "It has to be Roger Bellair."

"Roger Bellair?" I asked. "Why would he want to hurt Harmony?"

"Think about it. If he's still in love with Sydney," Claudia explained, "he'd want her to have all the best assignments. So he'd have to get Harmony out of the way."

"But we're not even sure if he's in love with Sydney," I said.

"Maybe he's not," said Claudia. "In that case, maybe he meant the poison for her.

Maybe he's bitter over being rejected by her. Either way, I bet he's the culprit."

"I don't know," I said slowly. "I can think of a few other people with motives."

"Who?" asked Mal. "Other models, you mean?"

I nodded. "Like Cynthia Rowlands," I said. "Maybe she's jealous of all the attention Harmony's been getting."

"Or what about that one you mentioned — Blaine Gilbert?" asked Mary Anne, joining in. "Didn't you say she was pretty ambitious?"

I nodded. I'd passed on all of Cokie's gossip. "That's true," I said. I thought for a moment. "Know what, you guys?" I asked. "We really have our work cut out for us if we want to solve this mystery. From what I've seen so far, almost *anyone* involved in Fashion Week could be a suspect."

Suddenly, the week ahead seemed a whole lot more exciting — and quite a bit scarier.

CHAPTER 6

Sunday

Abby, I think you handled things really well today. If I'd been the one to catch those kids, I'm not sure I would have known what to do.

Of course you would have, Jessi. And it wasn't as if I handled things all by myself. You helped a lot. Anyway, I think we really made an impression on the kids.

Definitely. I don't think any of them will ever try something so stupid again.

While I was busy with that first crazy day of Fashion Week, Abby and Jessi were busy, too. Busy stopping a disaster before it happened. Disaster? I'll explain. It happened while they were sitting for Stoneybrook's version of the Brady Bunch: the Barrett-DeWitt kids.

The Barrett kids have been BSC clients for quite awhile. Buddy's eight, Suzi is five, and Marnie's only two. Together, they used to be quite a handful. In fact, our nickname for them was "The Impossible Three." When we first met them, their parents had just finalized their divorce, and the Barrett household was majorly disorganized.

Things improved when Mrs. Barrett met Franklin DeWitt, a father raising four kids on his own. The DeWitt kids all look something like their dad, who's tall and thin with auburn hair. Lindsey, who's eight, is the oldest. Then comes Taylor. He's six. Madeleine is four, and Ryan, the youngest, is two.

Now that Mrs. Barrett and Mr. DeWitt are married, the kids are part of one big family. And after a period of adjustment, they've even learned to live pretty happily together. But, as you can imagine, the seven kids together are too much for one sitter to handle alone. In fact, we have a BSC rule about that: four or more kids means more than one sitter. We always send two sitters to the Barrett-DeWitt house.

Even two sitters sometimes feel overwhelmed. That was the state Jessi and Abby were in on Sunday afternoon. It was a bright, sunny day — one of the first really good days of spring — and the kids were, to put it nicely, in high spirits. (Abby didn't put it quite so nicely when she told me about her day. I think she said something about the kids "bouncing off the walls.")

The first fifteen minutes of the sitting job were devoted strictly to damage control.

"Suzi, put the gerbil back in its cage," Abby said.

"Buddy, please stop throwing that ball in the house," said Jessi.

"Lindsey, are you sure your dad doesn't mind you playing with his golf clubs?" Abby asked.

"Madeleine, I don't think that lipstick belongs to you, does it?"

"Taylor, no more Popsicles for you today. And please find a sponge and wipe up that spill."

"MARNIE! NO!"

"Ryan, both hands out of the goldfish bowl!"

Jessi and Abby looked at each other in despair. "Okay, time out, everybody," Abby said, whistling through her teeth and putting her hands in a T formation. "Let's take a little

51

break while we figure out something fun to do together today."

Jessi and Abby herded the kids into the den and sat them down.

"It's a beautiful day," Jessi said. "I think we should spend the afternoon outdoors."

"Doing what?" asked Taylor, looking bored.

"There's nothing to do in our stupid yard," added Suzi.

"*Hate* outside!" Ryan said, folding his arms.

"Don't be silly," said Abby. "There's always plenty to do outdoors. We could take a nature walk, for example. Or help weed the flower beds. Or — "

"BO-ring," interrupted Lindsey.

"Well, what would you suggest?" asked Abby, trying not to be offended.

"I suggest we forget the whole thing and watch wrestling on TV instead," said Buddy with a devilish grin.

"I mean, what would you suggest we do *outdoors?*" Abby said.

"Take the TV outside and watch it there?" asked Buddy.

Abby snorted. "Obviously, you want your baby-sitters to come up with a fun activity. All right, then, here it is." She leaned over and whispered into Jessi's ear. Jessi smiled and nodded and whispered back.

"Today will be the First Annual Barrett-

DeWitt Family Field Day," Abby announced. "Get ready to run your fastest, jump your highest, and throw your farthest."

"Do I have to — " Suzi began, but Jessi interrupted her.

"Yup," she said. "Everybody has to participate. Otherwise, how will we know who's really the best in each event? And you don't want to miss the prizes, do you?"

Suzi's eyes lit up. "Prizes?" she asked.

"Of course," said Abby, taking a quick mental inventory of her Kid-Kit. She hoped she had enough stickers and markers to hand out to the winners.

The kids started to sound a bit more enthusiastic, so Jessi and Abby began to round up sweaters and sneakers for everyone. After a quick snack, they headed outside, into the backyard. It's not a big yard, but Abby and Jessi were creative. Buddy helped Abby find a softball, a basketball, and some ropes for marking off distances for races. Lindsey and Jessi, meanwhile, prepared a long-jump area next to the garage, then looked around for other sports equipment the kids could use.

It didn't take long to set up the events, and soon the First Annual Barrett-DeWitt Family Field Day was under way. With Abby as organizer and referee and Jessi as head coach and cheerleader, the kids couldn't help having fun, no matter how reluctant they'd been earlier.

The first event, Abby announced, would be a relay race between two teams made up of the older kids. Lindsey and Suzi were on one side, and Taylor and Buddy were on the other. When Abby gave the word, the first kids on each team raced around the yard until they came to the swingset. There, they handed off their "batons" — over-filled water balloons — to their teammates. The water balloons were Abby's idea, and they added a lot of laughter and screaming to the race. Taylor was soaked by the time he crossed the finish line because he'd gripped his too tightly. Suzi's balloon, on the other hand, made it through the race without bursting. To celebrate, she threw it in the air — and it landed with a splash. On Jessi. The kids thought that was just hilarious.

Next, Abby announced an event for the little kids. "Time for the Mini-Marathon!" she said as she helped Madeleine, Ryan, and Marnie line up for their race. "Run as fast as you can to the apple tree and back. No, wait, Ryan! Not until I say go. Okay, are you all ready? Do you have to go to the potty, Marnie? Okay, everybody hold on while I take Marnie to the bathroom."

Finally, after a few more false starts, the race was on. Jessi and Abby giggled and cheered as they watched the little kids make their way across the yard and back. Madeleine was a lot faster, but she fell behind when she was distracted by a pink tulip in the garden, and Marnie and Ryan kept on going.

Marnie was declared the winner, and Jessi gave her a kitten sticker. She also gave Madeleine and Ryan puppy stickers, just to head off any temper tantrums. After all, second and third places are very important, too.

"Everybody ready for the next event?" asked Abby, looking around. "Hey, where are Lindsey and Buddy?"

Jessi looked around, too. "They were here a minute ago."

"I saw them go that way," said Taylor, pointing toward the toolshed.

"I'll go find them," Abby said. "Why don't the rest of you start practicing your long jumps?" She headed toward the toolshed, figuring that Buddy and Lindsey must be inside looking for more sports equipment.

They weren't inside. But Abby heard voices and, following the sound, found the kids behind the shed. "Hey, guys," she said. "What's up?"

"Abby!" said Buddy, looking very white. He stuck his right hand behind his back.

Lindsey looked pale, too. She put her left

hand behind her back. "Um, hi, Abby," she said.

Abby had the feeling that she'd caught them at something. "Want to tell me what you guys were doing?" she asked.

"N-nothing," said Buddy.

"Just . . . nothing," Lindsey added.

"Then what are you hiding behind your backs?" asked Abby. "Come on, let's see."

Slowly, slowly, Buddy brought his hand around and opened it up. Lying in his palm was a cigarette.

Lindsey reluctantly showed Abby the pack of matches she was holding.

At first, Abby was speechless. She told me later how shocked she was. ("I nearly blew a gasket," she said. "But I didn't want to yell at them. So I asked questions instead.") "But where — why — ?" she began, finally.

"I took it from Franklin's briefcase," Buddy admitted. Abby remembered hearing that Mr. DeWitt was a longtime smoker, and that although Mrs. Barrett was always after him to quit, he hadn't been able to yet.

"We just wanted to try it," added Lindsey.

"The ads make it look so cool," Buddy said. "And it looks neat when people do it in the movies."

"So you haven't smoked yet?" asked Abby, momentarily relieved.

They shook their heads. "This was going to be our first one," said Buddy, holding up the cigarette and looking at it a little wistfully.

"Does that mean we're not in trouble?" Lindsey asked.

"Not in trouble?" asked Abby. "You must be joking. You are in *major* trouble. Your parents are going to hear about this."

"Do you have to tell them?" asked Lindsey, looking alarmed.

"Absolutely," said Abby. "In fact, everybody's going to hear about this." She held out her hand for the cigarette and matches, then told Buddy and Lindsey to follow her. She marched them back to the spot where Jessi was standing with the other kids and announced what she'd discovered.

The kids and Jessi looked shocked.

Buddy and Lindsey looked ashamed.

"Let's all sit down and talk about smoking," Abby said. "I think we need a little education around here." She told the kids how smoking affects your lungs, your entire body, your health, and the health of people around you. "I could have a really bad asthma attack if I had to breathe someone's secondhand smoke," she noted. She talked about peer pressure and about how many smokers begin when they're young. She went on and on, until Buddy interrupted with a question.

"But isn't it okay if you only smoke a few a day?" he asked. "That's what I've heard some grown-ups say."

"*None* a day is the only okay way," Jessi replied. "Do you think I could be a ballet dancer if I smoked cigarettes?" She told the kids how athletes need to have clean lungs and strong hearts.

The kids were listening with their full attention. Jessi and Abby took turns telling them everything they knew about smoking and why it was definitely not a good idea for kids *or* adults. By the end of the afternoon, they were sure they'd convinced not only Buddy and Lindsey but the whole Barrett-DeWitt clan that smoking was uncool. One disaster prevented before it happened — courtesy of the BSC.

CHAPTER 7

"You look *fine*," said Claudia impatiently as I checked myself in the mirror one last time. "Come on, we're going to be late."

It was Monday afternoon, and the last bell had just rung at school. Claudia and I were planning to head to Bellair's together. It was time for the first day of the catalog shoot.

I was nervous about it. I've done a little posing in front of cameras before but never for a national catalog. I wanted to be sure I looked my absolute best.

The night before, I'd spent hours figuring out the best outfit to wear. I knew I wouldn't wear my own clothes in the photos, but I wanted to make a good impression on the art director, the photographer, and Mrs. Maslin. I'd narrowed my choices down to a pink wool jumper, a plaid skirt and white shirt, and a navy blue suit with tailored pants. Then I'd modeled each outfit for my mom, and together we'd decided on the pink jumper, with the white shirt from the other outfit.

I'd also put a lot of thought and time into my hair and makeup. Now I touched up the lip gloss and checked once more to make sure my mascara wasn't smeared. "All right," I said. "This'll have to do."

"They'll love you," said Claudia. "Now let's *go*. If I'm late, Roger Bellair will give me a hard time, and I don't need that." She slung her backpack over one shoulder and pulled me along.

Claudia didn't seem too concerned about *her* appearance, but as usual she looked awesome. She was wearing one of her "working artist" outfits: a pair of white jeans with drips and squiggles of colorful paint all over them, a smocklike denim shirt, her favorite red high-top sneakers, and a hairdo that said "creative" — a loose bun held in place by two red lac-quered chopsticks.

I knew she was also nervous about this first day of the photo shoot. But she couldn't be as jittery as I was. After all, she'd be behind the cameras, not in front of them. I wondered whether any of the other models were anxious.

We arrived at Bellair's a little early. (Kristy has trained us baby-sitters to be ultra-punctual.) And right away I saw that none of the other models seemed nervous at all. Or if they were, they were awfully good at hiding it. The noise volume in the dressing room was as high as it had been the day before, as girls ran back and forth between makeup artists, hair stylists, and wardrobe people. Harmony, looking recovered from her poisoning, was among them. But I noticed that she held herself apart from everyone else, avoiding the gossip and turning down offers of diet soda or cigarettes.

Claudia wished me luck, reminded me to keep my eyes peeled for suspicious activity, and took off to find Roger Bellair. Alone, I took a quick peek in the mirror. I looked just as sophisticated as some of the older models, I thought. I was sure I'd make a good impression on the catalog people.

I would have, too.

Except for the fact that they never saw my hair, my perfect makeup, or my pink wool jumper.

Seconds after Claudia left, someone grabbed my shoulder and pulled me over to a dressing table. It was Monica, one of the makeup artists. "Okay," she said, "off with your clothes and into this smock."

"But — " I began.

"But nothing," she said. "Do you want foundation all over that nice white shirt? Come on, let's go! I have four girls to do after you."

I pulled off my jumper and shirt and put on

a beige smock she held out for me. Then she sat me down and, using makeup-removal wipes, scrubbed off every bit of my carefully applied makeup. Then she slapped on about a *ton* of her own makeup, including foundation, powder, eyeshadow, lip liner, and gloss, and plenty of blush. This makeup job was a lot heavier than the one I'd had for the show. I could barely face myself in the mirror when she was done. I thought I looked *awful*.

"It's all for the cameras, hon," she said. "You need a lot, with the lights and all. It'll look great in the pictures. You'll see."

I barely had time to answer, because just then, one of the hair stylists, Jacqui, took Monica's place. "Nice 'do," she said, as she pulled my beautiful French twist to pieces. "But Julio is looking for a more natural look. 'Wind-swept,' he told me."

Julio was the art director. He and Jamie, the photographer, were the ones I'd wanted to impress with my personal sense of style. But Julio had his own ideas about how he wanted me to look. I realized something then that might seem obvious. Modeling is not about a personal sense of style. It's about being able to change into whoever somebody else wants you to be.

And I wasn't crazy about the girl Julio and

Jamie wanted me to be. By the time I was ready for my first pose of the day, I barely recognized myself. I was so made up that I could have passed for forty. My hair was teased and tossed until it looked as if I'd slept on it for a week. The clothes were all right — Bellair's usually carries nice things — but they weren't ones I would have picked out for myself. The jeans were too trendy, the top was too tight and short, and as for platform shoes? I'll never understand why people like them. To me they just look clunky.

But hey, I told myself, *this is the wonderful world of fashion.*

The entire transformation had only taken about twenty minutes. Everybody in that dressing room seemed to be in a tremendous hurry. But then I found out another basic thing about modeling: It involves a lot of standing around. Ever heard the expression "hurry up and wait"? Well, that's what I — and every other model — ended up doing that day.

There we were, a gaggle of gorgeously groomed girls. Going nowhere. We stood around for awhile. Then we gave up and *sat* around for awhile. Most of the girls passed the time by taking frequent "ciggie breaks," while the rest of us had nothing to do but examine our cuticles. Of course, I was also examining my fellow models for signs of guilt — but not one of them did anything even remotely suspicious.

Boring? That's an understatement.

I couldn't understand what was taking so long, until I watched the shoot before mine. Then it all became clear. The thing was, for every finished shot, the photographer probably used three rolls of film. And before he could even take a single picture, he had to reposition the lights (or rather, his assistant had to), load the camera (or tell his assistant to load it), and take some Polaroids to see whether the setup was correct (and give them to his assistant to hold).

It may sound as if Roger Bellair, the assistant, ended up doing all the work. Not true. He had Claudia to order around, remember? Both of them scurried here and there, ignoring everything but Jamie's commands.

Actually, Jamie was working just as hard as anyone else. His job as photographer also included talking to the models, putting them into position, and flattering them just enough so that they'd perform the way he needed them to.

I watched him as he set up a group shot with Cynthia, Harmony, and Cokie. First, he and Julio conferred quietly about what they wanted for a finished product. Then he talked to the girls, telling Cynthia to put her hand on her hip, Harmony to smile and toss her head — "Yes! Just like that!" — and Cokie to relax and try to look natural. Once he had posed them, he took some Polaroids, and he and Julio conferred again. Then he moved the girls around some more, changed the lighting one more time, and checked everything with his light meter. At the last minute, Julio insisted on changing Harmony's nail polish from hot pink to dusty rose. Then, finally, Jamie was ready to shoot.

Me? I was ready for a nap.

Twenty minutes later, Jamie told Cynthia, Harmony, and Cokie that he was done. "Okay, McGill and Rowlands, you're up next!" said Julio, checking his clipboard.

I turned around and saw Cynthia run back in, dressed in an outfit similar to mine. "I didn't know we were doing this together," I said.

"Neither did I," she said, smiling. "But I'm glad. It'll be more fun that way."

I couldn't help liking her when she said that. But I also couldn't forget that she was, like every other girl there, a suspect in the poisoning of Harmony.

She and I traipsed out into the lights. "Stace?" I heard Claudia call uncertainly. It was as if she didn't recognize me — and who could blame her? I shaded my eyes with one hand to cut the glare and waved when I caught sight of Claudia standing behind one of the light towers.

Julio and Jamie looked us over, conferred, and looked us over one more time. Then Jamie snapped out some instructions, and Claudia and Roger ran around moving equipment.

"Okay, girls, let's see you act like long-lost sisters who are thrilled to see each other again," said Jamie. "Smile, jump up and down, whatever," he added. His instructions were a little vague, but Cynthia and I tried to obey while he took a bunch of Polaroids. Then we let the smiles drop while he and Julio looked them over and conferred some more.

"Great, great," said Jamie finally. "Terrific, McGill. And you, Rowlands, you're a natural. The camera loves you."

I felt a twinge of jealousy when he said that about Cynthia, but when I looked at the Polaroids afterward, I had to admit it was true. I looked okay, but Cynthia looked *great*.

By the time we'd finished, I was feeling exhausted. And I still had three more outfits to model! I ducked into the bathroom and did a quick blood test to find out whether I needed some insulin, but my numbers came up okay. As long as I could grab a quick bite, I'd be fine.

I headed back into the dressing room to find

my backpack, which held a snack I'd prepared at home. As I passed the shooting stage, Julio was calling for the "pajama party shoot." I knew that was one of the group shots, with Sydney, Harmony, and Blaine.

"Oh, no!" I heard someone cry as I rounded the corner. "This is so creepy! Who would *do* a thing like this?"

It was Blaine. She was holding up a piece of clothing that looked as if it once had been a pajama top: It was white cotton with pink roses.

It also happened to be shredded.

It hung in tatters, looking as if someone had gone at it with a very sharp pair of scissors. Someone mean, someone angry. Someone, I thought with a shiver, who might be out to hurt one of us.

CHAPTER 8

Sydney's red-and-white-checked flannel robe was shredded, too, and so was Harmony's tie-dyed baby-doll nightie.

And the three pairs of bunny slippers the girls were supposed to wear? You don't even want to hear about what was done to those poor things.

"Gross!" said Blaine, looking at one of her slippers. "Somebody around here has a really weird sense of humor."

"I'm not laughing," said Sydney.

Harmony wasn't laughing, either. Nor was she talking. She was just sitting there, white as a sheet. Looking at her, I had the peculiar feeling that she might actually know who had cut up her clothes — and that it was the same person who had poisoned her.

Then I shook my head and told myself I was being silly. If she knew, she'd tell security, or Mrs. Maslin, wouldn't she?

Speaking of Mrs. Maslin, she appeared on the scene just as Blaine and Sydney were starting to panic about what they were going to wear for the pajama party shoot, now that their clothes had been ruined.

"I mean, look at these!" Sydney was saying as she held up her pajamas. "Could they be any more useless?"

"Jamie is waiting for us," wailed Blaine. "What are we going to do?" She glanced around desperately, as if she hoped another nightgown might fall from the heavens.

"Don't worry, girls," Mrs. Maslin said soothingly, although I'd seen the shock in her eyes when she first glimpsed the shredded clothes. "The manufacturer sent plenty of samples. We're having more brought down right away. Go ahead and change now." She turned and saw Harmony sitting there as still as a mouse. "You, too, Harmony," she said, shooing her along. "And don't look so frightened. It's just somebody's idea of a silly joke."

"Ha, ha, ha." Somebody behind me was laughing a diabolical laugh — quietly, and right into my ear. I whirled around.

"Claudia!" I cried. "That's not funny. You scared me."

"Sorry," she said, grinning. "I couldn't resist." She was standing there with her arms full of pajamas and nightgowns. "Julio told me to bring these in here. I guess somebody didn't think the first set was quite their look, huh?" She nodded at Mrs. Maslin, who was holding up each piece of clothing in turn and clucking her tongue.

I tried to laugh, but somehow I couldn't. The shredded clothing gave me the creeps in a big way.

Claudia must have sensed what I was feeling. She handed over the clothes to Mrs. Maslin and then pulled me aside, behind a rack full of summer dresses. "Don't let it scare you," she told me.

"I'm trying not to," I said. "But it's sure beginning to look as if somebody doesn't like models very much."

Claudia glanced around to see if anyone was listening. "Okay, I think I have another suspect for our list," she began.

Just then, Mal and Mary Anne showed up. They were breathing hard as they rounded the corner, as if they'd run all the way from the Kid Center.

"Mal!" I whispered, grabbing her arm and pulling her into our hideaway. "What are you guys doing here?" I asked. "Aren't you supposed to be on duty?"

"We're on a break," she answered. "We just heard what happened. This is really serious."

"Wow! News sure travels fast around here," I said.

Mary Anne whipped out the mystery notebook. "I brought this along today," she said. "I had a feeling we might want it." She started to make a few notes about the shredded clothes.

"Claudia was just going to tell me about a new suspect," I said.

"Who?" Mary Anne asked eagerly, forgetting about the notebook.

"His name's Dylan Trueheart," said Claudia.

Why did that name ring a bell?

"He's some kind of agent," she continued.

Then I remembered. "He's the guy who discovered Cokie!" I said.

Claudia gave a little snort. "Figures," she said. "From what I hear, he's desperate for clients."

"So why is he a suspect?" I asked.

"I can't say, exactly," Claudia admitted. "It's just that there's something suspicious about him. He's always lurking around. You've probably seen him. He's that guy with the black ponytail and the mirrored sunglasses? And he seems to know everything about all the models."

Now that she described him, I knew I'd seen him around. He *was* kind of shady looking. "But why would he poison Harmony?" I asked.

"Or shred clothes?" added Mal.

Claudia shrugged. "Maybe he's trying to make the other models look bad, so Cokie — his client — looks good in comparison."

I rolled my eyes. "If he thinks *anything* he does could make Cokie into a supermodel, he's seriously out to lunch."

"Still," said Mary Anne thoughtfully, "Claudia has a point." She made a few notes in the mystery notebook. "We'll definitely have to keep an eye on him."

"What else can we do?" I asked.

"We should try to find the weapon," Mal said.

"Weapon?" asked Claudia.

"The scissors," Mal said. "The ones somebody used to cut up those clothes. I mean, on the detective shows they always look for the weapon. And when they find it, sometimes they solve the crime."

"Okay," I said, even though I wasn't convinced. "We'll look for the scissors. What else?"

Just then, we were interrupted by a shout. "McGill!" Somebody with a clipboard walked by, calling my name. It was time for me to prepare for my next pose. It was a bathing suit shot, so it wouldn't take me long to dress, but I knew I'd better start.

"Talk to you guys later," I whispered. "Keep your eyes peeled."

"You, too," said Claudia.

"And — be careful," Mal added.

I felt a shiver run down my spine. "I will," I promised. I said good-bye to my friends and headed for the bathroom, feeling shaky. I tried to calm myself. Was there really anything to be afraid of? Maybe I was nervous over nothing. I took a few deep breaths and felt a lot better.

Then I saw the note on the mirror.

It was scrawled in bright red lipstick. MIRROR MIRROR ON THE WALL, it said. WHO WILL BE THE NEXT TO FALL?

It wasn't addressed to me. It was just there, threatening anyone who happened to look at it.

I felt a little faint.

"Who is *doing* this?" someone asked, and I looked up to see Cokie staring at the note. A couple of other girls had come in, too. For once, there was no talking and giggling. Just a subdued murmuring and some nervous laughter.

"I don't know," I answered. "But I'm going to find out." I hate feeling scared. I promised myself to fight that feeling, to concentrate instead on catching the person who was trying to frighten me and every other model at Bellair's.

I had to work fast. First of all, there were only four days left in Fashion Week. That didn't leave much time. Second, if my mom found out what was going on, she'd probably make me quit modeling. Finally, I knew that if my friends and I didn't solve the mystery soon, somebody could get seriously hurt.

The pranks continued all that day and into the next.

That afternoon, Jamie discovered that somebody had been into one of his camera bags. Eight rolls of film had been exposed — which meant that half a day's work was wasted.

One of the models I didn't know nearly threw a fit when she discovered a huge spider in one of her shoes.

Blaine was somehow locked in the freight elevator. Nobody knew where she was until one of the lighting guys finally heard her pounding and yelling for help.

During Wednesday's fashion show, Harmony took a bad fall off the catwalk when a bright light flashed into her eyes. (She wasn't hurt, and she insisted she had fallen because she was wearing high heels — but I'd seen the flash of light.)

74

Another model broke out into a terrible, stinging rash after she applied some foundation from a jar she'd found on her dressing table.

And then there were the notes.

PRETTY IS AS PRETTY DOES, UNTIL PRETTY DIES! said the one written in eyebrow pencil on the schedule posted on the dressing room door.

BEAUTY KILLS, said another, traced in some spilled face powder on one of the dressing tables.

And finally, in lip liner on one of the stalls in the girls' bathroom, MODEL BEHAVIOR CAN BE HAZARDOUS TO YOUR HEALTH.

Finally, Mrs. Maslin couldn't pretend it was a joke anymore. She gathered the models together after Wednesday's show, and told us she would do everything she could to make sure we were safe. She sounded very reassuring. But she also asked us to stay alert, and to be sure to report any suspicious behavior to her.

That night, I had a hard time hiding my fears from my mother. I couldn't believe she hadn't heard about what was going on. After all, she works at Bellair's. But this was her busiest season, and I knew she had barely a moment to herself.

For a second, over our dinner of takeout Chinese food, I had the impulse to tell her I wanted to quit. Modeling was fun, but it wasn't worth dying for.

But then I opened my fortune cookie. YOU WILL KNOW THE ANSWER SOON, it said. How could I resist sticking with the mystery after that message?

CHAPTER 9

Tuesday

Announcing the birth of a Great Idea: This is a really good one, guys. And you know the most shocking thing? This idea wasn't even mine. I know, I know, it's hard to believe. But it's true. The kids came up with it on their own. Well, okay, maybe I helped just a smidgen. . . .

"Rock."

"That's right! It's a nice rock, too." Kristy smiled at Emily Michelle and turned the pebble over in her hand. "Where did you find it?"

Emily pointed to the big planters by their front door, which are filled with about ten million identical "rocks."

"Good for you," said Kristy, giving her little sister a squeeze. "What else can you find for me?"

It was Tuesday afternoon, and while I was dealing with the fashion show sabotage, Kristy was enjoying the sun while she baby-sat for her younger siblings and stepsiblings. They were all hanging out in the huge Thomas/Brewer yard. Kristy was lying in the fresh new grass under the apple tree, which happened to be in bloom, feeling, she told me later, as if the spring day had been made just for her. Birds were chirping, bees were buzzing, lilacs were scenting the soft air.

David Michael, who's seven and a half, was playing three-way catch with Karen, who's seven, and Andrew, who's four. They tossed a softball back and forth, working on their throwing and catching. Kristy kept an eye on their technique and gave them pointers once in awhile, but mainly she let them just fool around. After all, this wasn't an official Krushers practice session. Even though all three kids are on her softball team, Kristy knows when to act like a coach and when not to.

Meanwhile, Emily Michelle, who's two and a half, was keeping herself busy. She was exploring the yard thoroughly, and every time she made a new discovery she toddled back to tell Kristy about it or show her something she'd found.

Emily was born in Vietnam, and I don't know much about her life as an orphan before she came to live with Kristy's family. She's had a hard time learning to talk, partly because she only heard Vietnamese for the first couple of years of her life. Kristy and her family have worked hard with her, though, and word by word she's learning to speak English.

"Fower," said Emily Michelle, handing a dandelion to Kristy.

"Flower," Kristy corrected. "Can you say *flower*?"

"Fower," Emily repeated, grinning. "Pitty."

Kristy laughed. "You're right," she said, giving up on the language lesson. "It is a pretty flower."

Satisfied, Emily toddled off. Kristy leaned back on her elbows and looked up at the white apple blossoms and the blue sky. She knew it was too early to start thinking about all the things she wanted to do over summer vacation, but she couldn't help dreaming about barbecues and pool parties and —

"Uck," said Emily Michelle.

"Uck?" asked Kristy, snapping out of her dream. "What do you mean, 'uck'?"

Emily slowly opened her hand. Lying in her palm was something that was most definitely not a flower or a rock. "Uck," she repeated.

Kristy took a closer look and realized what it was. "Oh, yuck!" she cried.

Emily nodded. "Uck," she agreed happily.

"Put that down," said Kristy. "It's one of Watson's disgusting old smelly cigar butts. Oh, ew!"

Emily dropped it, startled by Kristy's reaction. For a second she screwed up her face and looked as if she were going to cry.

"Oh, it's okay," said Kristy, giving her a quick hug. "It's not your fault."

"What's not her fault?" asked David Michael. He and Karen and Andrew had gathered around, curious about what could be grossing out Kristy.

"This disgusting thing." Kristy nudged the cigar butt with the toe of her sneaker.

"Oh, ew, ew, triple ew!" cried Karen.

"Why does Daddy have to smoke those gross things?" asked Andrew. "I hate when he does that."

"Mom hates it, too," said David Michael. "Luckily, he doesn't smoke them that often. She won't let him smoke them inside, especially in the winter, when it's too cold to open the windows."

"So this butt was probably lying on the patio under the snow all winter," said Kristy. "Gross."

"I keep asking Daddy to quit cigars," said Karen sadly. "But he just won't. Doesn't he know smoking is bad for him? He already had a heart attack."

"He knows," said Kristy, putting an arm around Karen's shoulders. "But sometimes that's not enough. Some grown-ups have a hard time giving up smoking."

"Like Mr. DeWitt," put in David Michael. News had traveled fast about Buddy's and Lindsey's brush with cigarettes. "Lindsey says he's tried to stop, but he can't."

"Same with Mr. Milton," said Karen. "He works at my school. I always tell him he shouldn't smoke, and he tells me he wishes he had never started."

"That's a good thing for you guys to remember," Kristy said, unable to resist the chance to give them a lecture. "You know, most people start smoking when they're young. Then they wish they hadn't."

"I'll *never* start smoking," said Andrew. "Cross my heart." He made a sweeping gesture over his chest.

"No moke," said Emily, who had found a ladybug while the others were talking.

"I wish Daddy would quit those cigars," said Karen. "I mean, I bet if he could go a little while without one, he'd see that he didn't really need to smoke them at all."

"Like the Great American Smokeout," said Kristy, musing.

"The what?" asked David Michael.

"It's this day planned by a group called the American Lung Association," explained Kristy. "They had an assembly about it at school last year. What they do is ask smokers all over the country to promise not to smoke for just one day. Some people end up quitting forever."

"Why isn't there a Great Stoneybrook Smokeout?" Karen asked.

"There could be," said David Michael slowly. "Couldn't there?" he asked Kristy. "I mean," he continued, gathering steam, "why not? We could ask all the grown-ups to quit for one day — like, this Saturday, even! It'd be cool. We'll make them sign pledges — "

"And the kids could sign pledges, too," Karen added excitedly. "Saying they'll never even start smoking in the first place — "

"Mr. Spinoli might do it," Andrew put in.

That stopped everybody in their tracks. "Uh, who's Mr. Spinoli?" asked Kristy.

"You know," said Andrew. "Mr. Spinoli. The hardware store man. He stands out on the sidewalk. He smokes cigarettes all the time."

Kristy smiled. "Sure, Mr. Spinoli might do it," she said. "But you guys are talking about a big project. Are you sure we can organize it so fast?"

"Definitely!" said Karen, jumping up and down. "Let's call some other kids so they can come over and help."

Kristy told me later that the kids' enthusiasm was contagious. She and her charges went inside and started to make calls, and an hour later a planning session was in full swing.

Buddy and Lindsey were there, and so were Jessi and her younger sister, Becca, who's eight. Abby had come along, bringing the kids she was sitting for: James, Johnny, and Mathew Hobart. Mrs. Hobart had been able to give them a ride. Mary Anne had arrived last, along with eight-year-old Charlotte Johanssen, who's one of the BSC's favorite charges.

Everybody gathered under the apple tree. Kristy had brought out a pad and pencil, and as the kids started tossing ideas around, she wrote them down. Some of the ideas were a little silly — such as Karen's plan for arming kids with water pistols they could shoot at anyone they saw smoking — but most of them were terrific.

"We should give out free gum," suggested Buddy. "Franklin always chews a ton of gum when he's trying to stop smoking."

"We can make buttons for the people who sign the pledge," said James. "That way everybody will know who they are, and we can tell them how great they're doing all day."

"I bet even Aunt Cecelia would sign the pledge," said Becca.

"Aunt Cecelia smokes?" asked Mary Anne. "I didn't know that."

"Not many people do," said Jessi. "She doesn't smoke a lot, and she never does it in public. She just sneaks one once in awhile. But I bet Becca's right. If we ask her, she'll try quitting for a day."

"So will Mr. Spinoli," said Andrew.

"And Mr. Milton," added Karen. "And Watson, definitely."

"And our mom," said James Hobart. "She's always saying she wishes she could quit."

Kristy was making a list of names. "I'll create a pledge form on my computer," she said. "We can print up a lot of copies and hand them out to every smoker we know."

"Don't forget the kids' pledge, too," said David Michael. "I bet every kid in my class will sign that one."

"Mine, too," said Becca. "Especially since your mom did that special assembly about how bad smoking is for you." She was talking to Charlotte, whose mother is a doctor.

Charlotte nodded. "My mom has lots of pamphlets and stuff, too," she said. "I bet she'd let us pass them out."

"Excellent, excellent, excellent," said Kristy, who had been writing so fast that her hand was cramping up. "I think the Great Stoneybrook Smokeout is going to be a great success."

Emily Michelle smiled up at her. "No more uck," she said.

At that, everybody cracked up. In three little words, Emily Michelle had summed up their entire goal.

CHAPTER 10

Thursday

Tea. It seems like such a boring beverage. But maybe there's something we can learn from it, and I don't mean by reading tea leaves. . . .

By Thursday, my friends and I had decided to step up our efforts to solve the mystery at Bellair's. We'd talked at our Wednesday meeting about everything that had happened, about suspects, about clues. Then we'd each chosen a clue or a suspect to follow up more thoroughly, and we'd agreed to write down all our findings in the mystery notebook.

Were we on the ball? Definitely.

Did we solve the mystery? Well . . .

The point is that we worked hard at *trying* to solve it. And maybe we came a little closer.

I'd chosen to investigate that first incident, when Harmony was poisoned. (No matter what Mrs. Skye said, I was still convinced that it *had* been a poisoning.) For example, how could I be sure that the tea really had been meant for Harmony? The cup she'd been drinking from was identical to every other cup on the catering table. For all I knew, the poisoner might have been trying to make someone else — one of the other girls who likes tea — sick. Or maybe it was just a random poisoning. That thought still made me feel queasy. It meant that somebody had just wanted to poison a model, any model. It could have been me.

I decided to spend some time near the catering table, so I could scope out who drank tea and who didn't. Maybe, by the process of elimination, I could figure out if anyone besides Harmony might have been the poisoner's target.

Luckily, I didn't have a very heavy modeling schedule that day. Julio only wanted me in one group shot for the catalog, and Mrs. Maslin had told us that since the fashion show that evening was highlighting maternity wear, she'd be using some of her older models. This gave me more time to investigate.

I'd already had my hair and makeup done, and my outfit — a flowery, ankle-length dress that I liked a lot — was hanging in the dressing room. I was ready whenever Julio called me. Meanwhile, I was free to lounge around in my jeans and a smock top.

I stationed myself near Gretchen, the smiling, energetic woman who'd been doing the catering all week.

"Need something to drink?" she asked me, waving a hand at the array of fruit juices, sodas, and bottled water on her table.

"No, thanks — " I began. Then I realized it might look suspicious if I hung out there without drinking anything, so I started again. "Actually, sure. I'll have some water." Regular soda was out, because of my diabetes, and I didn't feel like a diet soda or a hot drink. Especially tea.

Gretchen told me to help myself. I took a bottle of water and settled into a folding chair next to the table.

"Going to be here for a few?" Gretchen asked.

I nodded.

"Mind watching things?" She smiled. "I have to run out for more diet soda. I can't seem to keep enough in stock." She gave a rueful laugh. "Like any of you really need to diet," she added. "I'm the one who should be drinking the stuff."

"You look great," I told her. It was true. She may not have been a beanpole like Sydney, but she had a nice figure. "And I'll be glad to watch things." Glad? I was thrilled. It was the perfect excuse for spying on the drinking habits of my fellow models. "Take your time," I added.

Gretchen left, and almost immediately my first "customer" showed up: Harmony. "Hi," I said. "How about something to drink? Some tea?"

Harmony made a face. "I don't know if I'll ever drink tea again."

"Oops, sorry," I said. "I should have realized. Do you want some juice instead?" I offered her a bottle, and she took it. "I like your outfit," I told her. She was wearing a long skirt with a cropped white T-shirt top.

"Do you?" she asked. "It's for the shoot." She didn't look too thrilled.

"I think some of the clothes are awesome," I said. "And modeling is cool. But I guess you're used to it."

"I guess I am," she said, sounding bored. "Well, thanks for the juice." She saluted me with the bottle and wandered off. I watched her go. She seemed so listless. I wondered if it had something to do with the poison. Maybe she was still feeling under the weather.

Sydney showed up next, and although I offered her tea, she wouldn't take any. "My skin really reacts if I drink anything but water," she said, tossing her hair back. She walked off, after grabbing a bottle of water, without saying anything else.

Then came Blaine, Cokie, and Cynthia, in that order. Not one of them seemed tempted by tea. (I was starting to wonder if everyone was avoiding the tea on purpose, because they were nervous about being poisoned.) Blaine and Cynthia grabbed diet sodas, and Cokie did, too. I had a feeling Cokie was just drinking the stuff because all the other models did. I hoped that didn't mean she would also start smoking. Cokie might not be my best bud, but I'd hate to see anyone take up such a nasty habit.

"Mason! Gilbert!"

"That's us," said Cokie. "I guess they're

ready for our shoot." She preened a little, showing off her flowered short-shorts. "I'm in two group shots today," she said, "and I have one close-up, for a hair accessories shot."

Big whoop.

"Plus, I hear I have some excellent assignments for the final show," she added. "My agent is making sure of that."

Blaine and Cynthia just rolled their eyes, which is the only proper response to the kind of bragging Cokie was doing. Then Blaine tugged on Cokie's arm. "Let's go," she said, "or else they'll find somebody else for all those 'excellent' assignments."

As soon as they left, Cynthia leaned toward me. "Stacey," she said, "can I talk to you?"

I was so involved with the mystery that I thought she must be about to tell me she knew who'd been pulling the pranks. "Of course," I said, leaning forward.

"I have this problem," she began.

"Yes?"

"It's just that . . . that I don't really know if I want to keep on modeling or not," she said, looking down at her hands. "I mean, I know most girls would *kill* to be in my position — "

We looked at each other, a little shocked at what she had just said. "I don't mean like poisoning Harmony," she said quickly. "I don't know anything about the stuff that's been going on. I just mean that I know other girls would be envious. But sometimes I think I'd like to chuck it all and just have a normal life. I mean, school and giggling in the hallways. Sending notes to boys. Going to basketball games. I miss those things."

I nodded, sympathetic but secretly disappointed. I'd been hoping for a clue. "Maybe you should quit modeling for awhile," I suggested. "I mean, you can always go back to it. You're only sixteen. If you took time off you could concentrate on your life and your friends."

We talked for quite awhile. I talked about school and friends and the BSC. She talked about modeling, and how it was fun and exciting at first but how it was starting to feel like a drag. "After all, it's work," she said. "And I'm not sure I'm ready for a full-time job."

By the time Gretchen returned, I'd learned a lot. Not about the mystery, or about who else the poisoner might have been after, but about Cynthia and the real world of modeling. I was sorry I hadn't come any closer to solving the mystery, but I was glad about one thing.

I'd begun to make a new friend.

Well, I spent all my time wacthing mr. Im - The - Bossie's - Son, and I can tell you one thing for shur. He may not be our prime suspect, but hes defenetly a prime jerk.

Claudia had decided to keep a close eye on Roger Bellair. Since she worked with him, that wasn't too hard. She'd been suspicious of him because of his connection to Sydney, but until that afternoon she hadn't known much about his personality. He worked hard during the shoots. Claudia thought he wanted to impress Jamie. But when she started to follow him, Claudia began to see another side of Roger Bellair.

The jerky side.

The side that never let anyone forget he was the boss's son, and that someday he would inherit Bellair's. As he cruised through the store, Claudia noticed that he ordered people around as if they were slaves. "That display is a mess," he told a clerk in the men's department. "Fold those shirts and tidy it up." He treated Gretchen as if she were his personal cook. He told off one of the elevator operators for closing the doors too quickly. And he acted as if all these people should be calling him Prince Roger.

Claudia was grossed out, but by the end of the day she felt pretty confident about crossing Roger off the suspect list. "After all," she reasoned, "if he *did* want to help or harm Sydney's career, wouldn't he use his status at the store? I mean, he'd just have her fired, or have all the other models fired, or whatever."

I had to agree that she was probably right. But I urged her to keep an eye on him anyway. It never pays to cross off a suspect too early.

Okay. I admit I was fooled. But wouldn't you be, if you saw all those secret conferences going on?

Mary Anne was keeping an eye on Dylan Trueheart. Of course, she could only follow him when she was on a break from the Kid Center. Fortunately, there weren't too many kids to care for that afternoon, so she and Mal were able to slip away a few times.

The first "secret conference" Mary Anne saw was between Cokie and Dylan Trueheart. They were whispering away in a corner when Mary Anne passed them. Next, she saw the agent chatting with Blaine Gilbert. Were they hatching a plot? Mary Anne knew that Blaine was ambitious. Was she ambitious enough to join

Dylan Trueheart in pulling a series of scary pranks?

As it turned out, the answer was — probably not. Instead, Mary Anne found out, the secret conferences had to do with modeling assignments, and who was going to land which ones for the big show. How did she find out? By eavesdropping on one more conference, the one between Dylan Trueheart and Mrs. Maslin. He was "unofficially" representing Blaine, he told her, and wanted to make sure that both she and his other client, Cokie, were "treated well" when the time came to decide which models would wear which clothes. It was all just a part of the heavy competition going on all the time, Mary Anne concluded. She couldn't say for sure that Dylan Trueheart was innocent but it certainly looked that way.

I found it! I found it! I found it! Did I mention that I found it?

Mal was the only one of us who hit pay dirt with her investigation. Can you guess what she found? That's right: "the weapon." The scissors that had been used to cut up the clothing were right where the cutter must have thrown them, behind a pile of boxes near the spot where the pj's and bunny slippers had been viciously attacked. They were junky old scissors, spotted with what looked like pink paint and patches of rust, but they were very sharp. How did Mal know they were "the weapon"? Because they still had shreds of flannel clinging to the blades. There was no question about it. But there was one other question, one that each of us had raised about our investigation. Mal put it best, at the end of her entry in the mystery notebook.

Okay, so I found it. Now what do we do?

CHAPTER 11

What we did was nothing. By the end of Thursday's Fashion Week activities, we were completely exhausted. I, for one, was ready for a hot bath and a hot date — with my mom, a bowl of popcorn, and a movie on the VCR. I needed to veg for a few hours and forget about everything that was happening at Bellair's. I mean, I didn't mind the modeling part, though I was pretty sure I wouldn't want to make a career out of it, but the mystery was driving me bonkers.

During my bath, I realized something. Nothing horrible had happened that day. No spiders in shoes, no poison. Oh, there'd been a lipstick note on the bathroom mirror when we'd arrived, but those notes were beginning to seem routine. I was almost tempted to tell myself that everything had been blown out of proportion, that nobody was after me, that it was all just a series of silly pranks — and that the prankster had finally become bored.

Then Friday rolled around and I was nearly killed.

Well, maybe that's putting it a little dramatically. But if you'd been there, you'd know that what happened *was* pretty dramatic. I'll back up and tell the whole story, and you'll see what I mean.

As my friends and I split up at Bellair's front door on Friday afternoon, we promised each other we'd keep up the detective work. Time was running out; we had to work fast. Mal was hoping to find more clues that would connect "the weapon" to whoever it was who had sliced, diced, and shredded those pj's. Claudia was going to continue to keep an eye on Roger Bellair, even though she was pretty sure he was innocent. ("Jerky, but innocent," was how she put it.) Mary Anne was still thinking that Dylan Trueheart might be behind the pranks. There was just something sneaky about the way he operated, according to her. And me? I was going to concentrate on my fellow models, wondering which one might be ambitious enough to be willing to terrorize the rest of us.

Ten minutes after I'd arrived, I was sitting at the dressing table while the hair and makeup people fussed over me, preparing me for that day's catalog shoot. Monica was giving me a sixties look, with plenty of dark eyeliner and this wild, almost white, lipstick. Jacqui teased my hair until it was puffy, then teased it some more. They were transforming me completely, but I was barely paying attention. Instead, I was checking out the other models.

Harmony was already made up. Her hair was done, and she was dressed in what I figured was her first outfit for the photo shoot. The shoot that day featured retro clothes — the mod, sixties look — and Harmony was wearing a neon paisley miniskirt, white go-go boots, and a fluffy white jacket made of very fake fur. As I watched, Harmony's mom tugged at the hem of her miniskirt. "It's too short," she said.

"Mom, it's fine," said Harmony.

"I'm telling you, it's too short. Isn't this too short?" Harmony's mom had grabbed Mrs. Maslin, who was trotting by with her clipboard.

"It looks fine to me," said Mrs. Maslin, barely slowing down.

"I still say it's too short," insisted Harmony's mom.

Harmony rolled her eyes and stomped off.

"Where are you going?" her mother asked. "Young lady — " But she was too late. Harmony had disappeared. I couldn't blame her for wanting to escape, if her mom was going to act like that.

Meanwhile, Sydney was the definition of calm. I realized, as I surreptitiously watched her, that I'd never seen her seem particularly excited or nervous or bent out of shape about anything that went on around her. Even those slashed pajamas had hardly phased her. She always maintained this very aloof, cool attitude. Sydney was a pro.

She was sitting two chairs down from me, chatting softly on a cellular phone while a makeup person painted her nails. I wondered who she was talking to. Was it Roger Bellair's replacement? There was no way I'd know, since Sydney wasn't the type to share secrets.

In the chair next to me sat Cynthia Rowlands. She was paging through a shiny pamphlet, and when I looked over at her she smiled and held it up to show me what it was. *The Hackett School*, it said on the front, over a picture of happy students sitting in a circle under a tree.

Cynthia definitely seemed to be leaning toward giving up modeling for school. I wondered if Fashion Week would be her last professional job for awhile.

Blaine Gilbert was dressed and made up already. She stood off to one side, talking intently with Dylan Trueheart. I studied Blaine, trying to figure her out. She and I had a couple of things in common. We both called Stoneybrook home, and we had both fallen into modeling without meaning to. But the similarities ended there. I knew that Blaine was far more ambitious than I'd ever be. She seemed to know that modeling was what she really wanted to do, and she seemed to be going after her goal full speed ahead. She was good at it, too. She was a real natural in front of the camera. I wasn't so sure that Dylan Trueheart was the best person to help her, but what did I know?

As I watched them, I saw Cokie waltz over to them and insert herself into the conversation. She, too, was already set for the shoot, and I could just tell that she thought she was the cutest thing around.

I noticed that Dylan Trueheart didn't seem too thrilled to see her, which gave me the feeling that Blaine Gilbert had replaced Cokie as his number-one client.

As I watched the three of them, Mrs. Maslin trotted into view, trailed by Emily. "Come on, Mom, please? Pretty please? I'll be good for . . . for the rest of my life!" Emily was pleading with her mom, and I would have bet my earnings from Fashion Week that I knew what she was begging for. A spot in the big show on Saturday.

Everybody was starting to focus on that

show. It was the final event of Fashion Week and the last chance for each model to be a star. Mrs. Maslin had been working all week putting together the show, and I knew she must be very close to making final choices about assignments, including the one for Princess Bellair.

Everybody knew that. Which was why all the models had been super-polite to Mrs. Maslin, and super-friendly to Emily. At least, they *acted* nice and friendly — until the moment Mrs. Maslin and her daughter left the room. It was all just a game.

Me? I didn't care too much about what assignments I received. Modeling was fun, but I had known by the end of the first day of Fashion Week that I didn't want to make a career out of it. So there was no reason for me to join in the cutthroat competition. Besides, I had better things to do with my time.

I had a mystery to solve.

And, as I gazed around the room, I realized that I was no closer to finding any answers. I mean, I'd just looked over the entire cast of characters, and I had no idea which one of them might be responsible for poisoning Harmony, or locking Blaine into the freight elevator, or pulling any of those other nasty pranks. My fellow models all had their competitive side, sure. But none of them seemed blood-thirsty enough to want to *hurt* another model physically in order to boost her own career.

Maybe Claudia was right, I thought. Maybe Roger Bellair was responsible after all. Or maybe Mary Anne was right, and Dylan True-heart was willing to do anything to help his clients.

"Okay, people, time to head on up and out!" Mrs. Maslin had to shout to be heard over the usual din.

"Up and out?" I asked Blaine. "What does she mean?"

"Didn't you hear?" Blaine answered. "To-day's shoot is on the roof of the store. It should be a gas."

If I'd heard, it hadn't registered. I hadn't been paying much attention to anything but my own thoughts about the mystery. But Blaine was probably right. A shoot on the roof would be something different, and fun.

Different, yes. Fun? Not exactly. Not unless you call a near-fatal accident fun.

We all trooped up to the roof, making a big parade of it. Mrs. Maslin led the procession, followed by Julio and Jamie, who were fol-lowed by their assistants and their assistants' assistants. (Roger Bellair and Claudia were among that crowd.) The lighting guys were next, then came the stylists, toting any supplies they might need to touch up a lip here, an eyebrow there. Finally, we models brought up the rear, led by Harmony with her mother, and Blaine with Dylan Trueheart (and Cookie close behind).

We emerged onto the roof, which was covered with tar paper and had a waist-high metal railing all the way around it. The sky was blue, the air was clear, and the view was — well, the view wasn't exactly stunning, since it was only of downtown Stoneybrook, but it was okay.

Being on the roof of Bellair's was not like being on top of the World Trade Center or the Empire State Building. When you're up that high, the cars on the streets look almost like ants, and all of Manhattan looks like a giant ant farm. But those buildings are very tall. Bellair's is only five stories high, so the cars on the street looked pretty much like cars, only smaller. Still, I felt a little dizzy when I went near the railing and looked over. I mean, five stories is a long way down.

Jamie and his crew had set up the cameras earlier, so the shoot began as soon as we were all on hand. Julio started barking out orders about which models he wanted where, the makeup people dashed around with powder puffs, and Mrs. Maslin hovered nearby, checking things off on her clipboard. There was a certain festive feeling in the air, probably due to the fact that we were in a new location.

In the first shot, Harmony and I were supposed to relax on some lounge chairs Julio's crew had brought up. "It's a tar beach kind of a feeling," said Julio. "You know, that's what city people call the roof. Tar beach. It's cheap, it's convenient, it's groovy."

Groovy? Whatever.

"But we're not wearing bathing suits," Harmony pointed out. "I wouldn't lie out on a lounge chair in an outfit like this."

"Good point," said Mrs. Maslin.

Julio looked a little put out. "Well, what do you suggest instead?" he asked.

"We could stand near the railing," said Harmony, "as though we were looking out at the view."

I was a little surprised to hear Harmony speak up so much. Maybe it had something to do with the fact that her mother had left to do some errands.

"I like it," said Mrs. Maslin.

Julio shrugged. "You're the boss," he said.

Harmony and I walked to the railing. We turned around to ask Jamie what to do next.

But we never had the chance.

I guess I must have leaned on the railing a

little too hard — or else Harmony did — because the next thing I knew, it wasn't there anymore.

It wasn't there, and Harmony and I were falling.

CHAPTER 12

We didn't die, of course. We didn't even plunge four stories, only to be miraculously saved by the awning over the front entrance.

All we did was fall onto another section of the roof, about a foot lower than the part we'd been standing on.

Not that it didn't hurt. I was shaken up pretty badly, and my wrist ached. I must have stuck out my hand to try to break my fall. Harmony and I sat where we'd landed, staring at each other. Her face was sheet white; she must have been in shock. Other than that, she seemed okay, except for a few small scrapes and scratches.

"Sorry," she whispered.

"Why?" I said. "It's not your fault the railing broke."

"Stace! Are you okay?" I looked up to see Claudia staring down at me. Claudia — and everyone else. The whole catalog crew and all the other models had rushed to the edge of the roof to see if Harmony and I had survived.

"We're both fine," I said. "Can somebody help us up?"

Jamie jumped right down and gave me a hand. Then he helped Harmony stand. By then, a couple of other people had climbed down onto our part of the roof. Mrs. Maslin was first, clucking like a hen as she brushed off Harmony's back. "Terrible, terrible," she said. "I should have known the roof was a bad idea."

Claudia, who was now standing beside me, gave me a hug. "Are you sure you're not hurt?" she asked. "Should I go find your mom?"

"No, really, I'm fine," I said.

Just then, as if she'd been summoned by the word "mom," Harmony's mother turned up. "Sweetie!" she cried, smothering Harmony in a huge hug. "What happened? Are you all right?"

"I'm fine," Harmony told her mother. "It was scary, but I'm fine."

"I'm going to look into suing the store," vowed her mother. "If they paid the proper attention to maintenance, this never would have happened." She waved a hand at the broken railing.

"It's not the store's fault," Harmony mumbled. "Somebody's after me. First the poison, then those notes — and now this."

Harmony's mom looked doubtful. So did Mrs. Maslin. I don't think either of them wanted to believe that the broken railing had been foul play. "Harmony has a very active imagination," said her mom to Mrs. Maslin, a little apologetically.

Harmony looked frustrated. "Mom, I'm trying to tell you — "

"What are we going to do here?" Julio interrupted, approaching Mrs. Maslin. "We're wasting money, paying all these people to stand around."

"You're right," said Mrs. Maslin. "We do need to finish the shoot. But not on the roof. Can your people move everything back down to the studio?"

Julio heaved a sigh. "If that's what you want," he said, "that's what we'll have to do."

"Good," said Mrs. Maslin. "And while you set up, we'll have a short meeting in the dressing rooms." She turned to face the models, who were still standing there staring at us. "I want everybody to join us downstairs," she said. "I'm ready to announce the assignments for tomorrow's show."

A murmur went through the crowd. (I saw that phrase in a book once, and it describes what happened up there on the roof perfectly.)

And the murmuring kept up as we all marched back down the stairs. I knew everybody was dying to find out who would be receiving the top assignments, including, and most especially, the one for the Princess Bellair role. I wasn't too concerned, though. I was a lot more interested in finding out who had loosened the screws on that railing.

Loose screws? That's right. As I'd followed the others back to the main roof, I couldn't help taking a closer look at the spot where the railing had given way. Sure enough, two large screws were lying nearby, two screws that had either popped out or had been *taken* out, leaving the bracket that held that part of the railing completely loose and ready to fall apart at a touch.

I thought about those screws as I followed the others downstairs. It seemed pretty obvious to me that someone had deliberately tampered with them. Someone who wanted to give a couple of models a really big scare. But who? And what would that person do next?

We gathered in the dressing room, a group of shaken-up models and concerned adults. Mrs. Maslin started to talk, and as usual she was able to smooth things over and help people calm down.

Once everybody felt a little more relaxed, Mrs. Maslin began to read the list of assignments for the big show. There weren't too many surprises. By then, everybody had begun to see which models seemed best for what clothes. And, despite all that heavy competition, the truth was that there were plenty of great assignments to go around. I was very happy with the ones Mrs. Maslin had given me: two evening gowns, one casual outfit, and a tennis outfit.

Finally, when she'd reached the end of her list, Mrs. Maslin paused. "And now," she said, "I'd like everyone to greet this year's Princess Bellair — Harmony Skye!"

I think I was the only one looking at Harmony as Mrs. Maslin said her name. I was sitting right next to her. So I was probably the only one who saw her face fall when she heard the news. A millisecond later, she was smiling again, as everyone turned around to look at her while they applauded.

Once I'd seen that expression cross her face I couldn't forget it. Why on earth would Harmony be disappointed to hear she'd been named Princess Bellair?

I thought about it as we finished the shoot. I thought about it some more as I changed into my own clothes at the end of the day. And I was still thinking about it as my mom drove my friends and me to Kristy's for a late-evening BSC pizza party.

We'd decided to get together that night, since Claudia and Mary Anne and Mal and I had not been able to attend BSC meetings all week. And when the four of us walked into the Thomas/Brewer kitchen, it felt like a family reunion. Of course, we'd seen each other in school, but we hadn't had time to talk about everything that had been happening that week.

We — the Fashion Week crew — had plenty to tell the others about the events at Bellair's. And they had plenty to tell us about plans for the Smokeout. Plus, we had to pay a lot of attention to the pizzas Kristy had ordered.

So, for the first half hour or so, all we did was pig out and gab a mile a minute. Then, once the pizza had disappeared, we settled down and began to talk more seriously about the mystery at Bellair's.

The mystery notebook had been passed around, and everyone had read it. (Nobody in the BSC can resist a mystery.) Kristy, Abby, and Jessi each had their own theory about what was going on.

"I'm still suspicious of Roger Bellair," said Kristy, who was working her way through a bowl of Ben and Jerry's Cherry Garcia. "I think you scratched him off the suspect list way too soon."

"But I've been keeping an eye on him," said Claud, "and I swear, he never does anything suspicious. I know for a fact that he was nowhere near that railing today, because I was with him the whole time we were setting up."

"That doesn't mean he didn't loosen the screws yesterday," said Mal. "I think Kristy's right. Everybody's a suspect until we're absolutely positive that he or she is innocent."

"I agree," said Jessi, "which is why I agree with Mary Anne about Dylan Trueheart. I think he and Cokie may be working together."

"What?" everybody asked at once. Mal nearly dropped her bowl of sorbet.

Jessi grinned. "I think they're in it together," she repeated. "It wouldn't be the first time Cokie pulled dirty tricks."

We had to admit she was right. "But Cokie wouldn't actually *hurt* anybody," said Kristy.

"That's just it," insisted Jessi. "Has anybody actually been hurt? No. I think somebody's just trying to scare the models. Why, I don't know. But my guess is that Cokie may be that somebody."

"Well, I have a different theory," announced Abby. She put down her empty bowl and folded her arms. "I think it's Julio."

"Julio!"

"That's the most ridiculous — "

"Why Julio?"

"Who is Julio, anyway?"

Everybody was talking at once, and Abby

grinned. "Julio's the art director," she reminded Jessi, who had asked. "And as far as why, well — why not? It could just as easily be him as anyone else. So I picked him, just for fun."

Everyone cracked up. Except for me. I was still thinking, thinking, thinking.

Mary Anne, sensitive as always, noticed. "You've been very quiet, Stacey," she said. "Is something wrong?"

I shook my head. "No, nothing's wrong," I said slowly. "But I think I know who's responsible for everything that's been happening. And if you're willing to help me," I said, looking around at my friends, "I think we can solve this mystery before it's too late."

CHAPTER 13

"What if nobody comes?" Mal whispered.

"Then we'll have to try Plan B," I whispered back.

"What's Plan B?" asked Claudia, also in a whisper.

"I'll figure that out when the time comes," I answered.

"Shhh!!! Somebody's coming!" Mary Anne hissed.

We all fell silent.

The door swung open, and I heard footsteps approaching. I crossed my fingers, hoping I was right. Hoping she wouldn't notice how, out of five stalls in the women's bathroom, four were locked. Hoping I'd know what to do and what to say.

I peeked through the crack between the door and the frame, careful not to move or make any sound at all. It was hard to see, but there was definitely someone standing in front of the mirror. I was holding my breath, and I'm sure my friends were holding theirs, too.

Then I heard this little sound, just a tiny "snick," and I bit my lip. Was that the sound I was waiting for? I peeked through the crack again and saw motion.

It was now or never. I could be wrong, but even if I was, what did I have to lose? I had to go with my hunch. I squinched my eyes shut tight for a second, then opened them. "Go for it," I told myself. In one quick motion, I pushed open the door of the stall I'd been hiding in.

I was right. That "snick" had been the sound of a lipstick tube being opened. And the motion I'd seen was the swoop of an arm, as that lipstick was used to write large red letters in the middle of the mirror. The message wasn't complete yet. So far it just said TONIGHT'S THE NI — .

Harmony met my eyes in the mirror, then turned to face me. "So, you caught me," she said tonelessly. She didn't even seem surprised.

I didn't feel as great as I'd thought I would. "Yeah, I guess I did," I said.

"I never meant to hurt anyone," she said.

"I know that. But you sure scared a few people, me included."

"Sorry," she whispered, looking down at her feet. Then she took a quick breath and looked back into my eyes. "What are you going to do?

Tell everyone? It's my word against yours, you know. You can't prove anything."

"As a matter of fact," I said, "I can. I have a few witnesses. Come on out, guys." I turned toward the stalls. One by one, my friends emerged.

"It worked!" cried Mal.

"At least we didn't get up at six for no reason," said Claudia. (She hadn't been happy about my insisting we arrive super-early at Bellair's, but I knew it was the only way we'd catch Harmony in the act.) She grabbed a paper towel and began to scrub the lipstick off the mirror.

"Are you all right, Harmony?" Mary Anne asked, placing a gentle hand on Harmony's shoulder.

At that, Harmony began to sniff. Then she started to cry. "How did you know it was me?" she asked between sobs.

"Do you really want to know?"

She nodded.

"Well," I said, "once I started to put it all together, it was obvious." I leaned against a sink and began to explain. "The thing that really tipped me off was the look on your face when Mrs. Maslin said you'd been named Princess Bellair."

"Ugh," said Harmony, frowning. "That was the last thing I wanted."

"Right," I said. "You're sick of modeling, aren't you? Just like Cynthia. But your mom won't let you quit. So you tried to convince her that modeling could be very, very dangerous." I watched Harmony's face closely. So far, this was just a theory of mine.

Harmony gulped and nodded, and I knew my theory was correct. "I remember the first time I saw you," I went on. "Cokie pointed you and your mother out, and told me that your mother wouldn't rest until you were a top model. But I never had the feeling that a modeling career was that important to *you*. I mean, you never seemed psyched about the clothes, or the great assignments Mrs. Maslin gave you, or anything."

Harmony was nodding. "I liked it at first," she whispered. "It was even fun, for awhile. Then I lost interest in it, but by then she — my mom — was really excited about me being a supermodel."

"So you poisoned yourself," I said.

My friends gasped, but Harmony just nodded. "I knew it wouldn't kill me," she said, "but I wanted to seem really, really sick. That's why I drank almost the whole cup."

"Those stomach cramps couldn't have been much fun," Mary Anne said sympathetically.

"They weren't," said Harmony. "They would

have been worth it, though, if my mom had let me drop out of Fashion Week."

"But she didn't," I pointed out. "So next, you started writing these notes everywhere. And putting spiders in people's shoes."

"And you were the one who cut up those clothes," Mal put in.

"That's right," I said. "Remember those pink spots on the scissors, Mal? Well, I had suddenly remembered that Harmony's nail polish was pink that day, too. That was a big clue."

"I hid those scissors," said Harmony, surprised.

"And I found them," Mal replied proudly. "Right near the scene of the crime."

I was watching Harmony's face and thinking. "You know," I said, "I remember looking at you that day and having this weird feeling that you knew who had cut up those pajamas. But at the time, I never would have thought it was you!"

"I think I even creeped myself out," said Harmony with a tiny grin.

"Well, I know you creeped me out when you loosened the screws on that railing," I said. "I thought I was going to be history when that thing let go."

"I knew the other roof was there. I knew I wouldn't be badly hurt. And I didn't even mean for it to happen to you. I was just hoping I would fall. Anyway, how did you know I'd loosened the screws?"

"I didn't at the time," I said. "But I saw the screws on the roof, and later I remembered you were the one who suggested we should do the shoot over by the railing, instead of on the lounge chairs. And then I remembered the way you looked at me and said 'sorry' after we'd fallen."

"Very impressive detecting," Mal whispered, giving me a grin and a nudge.

Harmony agreed. "I can't even pretend to be innocent," she said. "You have all the clues. And now you have witnesses," she went on, waving a hand at the others, "who've heard me say that I did all these things. And I did. I was responsible for everything."

For a second, we were all silent.

Then Mary Anne spoke up. "You have to tell your mother," she said. "You have to tell her you don't want to model anymore."

"I can't," said Harmony. "You don't understand. . . ."

"We'll help you," Mary Anne said, gently but firmly.

Harmony looked down at the floor. "And do we have to tell everybody what I did?"

I exchanged glances with my friends. We all seemed to feel the same way. "That's not necessary," I said. "As long as you promise to stop doing stuff like that."

"I promise," said Harmony, crossing her heart.

Just then, Cokie burst into the bathroom. "What are you all *doing?*" she cried. "Mrs. Maslin wants to do a run-through of tonight's show. We're supposed to be ready in fifteen minutes!" She ran to the mirror and began to inspect her makeup. "I don't know why Monica uses this foundation on me," she said to herself.

"We were just leaving," I told her. And with that, the five of us left Cokie alone in front of the mirror — which, thanks to Claudia's efforts, was clean.

As we walked toward the dressing room, Harmony grabbed my hand. "Thanks," she whispered. "For catching me, I mean. I know that sounds weird, but thanks."

I thought I understood what she meant.

She took a deep breath. "I have to talk to Mrs. Maslin," she said. "She should let somebody else be Princess Bellair, because I don't want to be. In fact, this show tonight is going to be the last one I ever do."

Wow. "Do you want me to go with you?" I asked.

"No, you go ahead and get ready for the run-through," she said. "And I know you guys," she gestured at Mal, Mary Anne, and Claudia, "have things to do, too. Go ahead. I'll be fine."

She sounded sure of herself. So my friends and I went our separate ways: Mary Anne and Mal to the Kid Center, Claudia to find Jamie and Roger Bellair, and I to my mirror.

Ten minutes later, just as I finished dressing, Harmony came into the room with a smile on her face. "All set," she said. "Mrs. Maslin said she was sorry to hear my decision, and she promised not to tell my mother until I've had a chance to talk to her. She said she'll give the princess role to Blaine — which is great — and she also told me that she finally broke down and agreed to let Emily be in the show. She's going to be a lady-in-waiting."

Harmony was talking so fast and so happily that she didn't even notice the warning look in my eyes. The look that said, "Watch out, your mother just came into the room."

For, sure enough, Mrs. Skye had shown up. And she'd heard at least part of what Harmony had said.

"Tell your mother *what?*" she asked. "And what is this about you not being the princess?" She'd folded her arms, and she looked angry, but she was speaking very calmly. *Too* calmly.

Harmony gulped. "It's just that — that — "

"Harmony, you can do it." I'd moved next to her, and now I whispered into her ear.

"Mom, I just don't want to model anymore," said Harmony, in a rush. "And I'm not going to, after tonight. That's final."

Mrs. Skye looked shocked. "But — but — " she began.

"No," Harmony interrupted, sounding determined. "I don't want to do it anymore, and you can't make me."

"This is utter nonsense," said Mrs. Skye.

I'd hoped she would be more understanding. "Modeling isn't for everyone," I put in. "I think tonight's going to be my last show, too."

Mrs. Skye looked at me without really seeing me, and it was clear that she was already trying to think of some way to make Harmony reconsider. Obviously, things weren't going to change overnight for Harmony. But at least she'd been honest about how she felt. There wouldn't be any more fake poisonings or lipstick messages.

Harmony was going to have to work this out the hard way, but I had no doubt that she *would* work it out. And, if she needed us, my friends and I would be there to help.

CHAPTER 14

Saturday

Becca and I had our doubts about whether Aunt Cecelia could make it through a whole day without sneaking a cigarette. Did she prove us wrong? Read the rest and find out.....

Jessi and Becca knew a lot more about Aunt Cecelia's smoking habits than Aunt Cecelia would ever have guessed. She was so sneaky about it, and so careful. But the fact was, they always knew when she'd had a cigarette.

"For one thing," Jessi told us later, after the Great Stoneybrook Smokeout, "you could always smell it — on her breath, on her hands, on her clothes. Ugh!"

For another thing, they'd both noticed a pattern to Aunt Cecelia's trips out to the garden in the Ramseys' backyard. There was the after-breakfast trip, the late-morning trip, the after-lunch trip. You see what I mean.

(In wintertime, according to Jessi, Aunt Cecelia would open her bedroom window and lean out, puffing away. Jessi could see the clouds of smoke from her bedroom window.)

Then there were the car trips, the excuses about needing to buy milk at the convenience store, and all the times Aunt Cecelia would push back her chair after dinner and say, "Hmm, I think I'll take a little stroll." If Jessi or Becca asked to go with her, she'd say she was "in the mood for solitude," and take off alone.

It wasn't that Aunt Cecelia was a sneaky person in general. She wasn't. Jessi knew that the main reason she snuck around with her cigarettes was that Mrs. Ramsey disapproved. She didn't want Aunt Cecelia smoking in the house, and she definitely didn't want Aunt Cecelia smoking in front of Jessi, Becca, and Squirt.

So Aunt Cecelia became a secret smoker.

She'd been a little surprised when Becca and Jessi approached her with the Smokeout pledge. "Heavens, girls, I hardly smoke at all!" she said. "Don't you have any *real* smokers to go after?"

That's when Jessi and Becca had presented her with a list of every cigarette she'd smoked over the last few days. (Even though they'd been at school during the day, they knew when she smoked. She stuck to her pattern.)

"Goodness," Aunt Cecelia had said, holding the list at arm's length so she could read it without fetching her glasses. She'd cleared her throat. "You girls have certainly done your research," she'd said with a little smile. "I suppose it wouldn't hurt me to try quitting for one day. Where's a pen?"

She'd signed the pledge.

But Jessi and Becca didn't trust her. They knew their aunt, and they knew that she had not one, but two habits that are hard to break: smoking and sneaking. Therefore, they decided in advance that they'd spy on her all day Saturday and shame her if they caught her with a cigarette. "She'd be so embarrassed if we caught her breaking her pledge," said Jessi. "She'd probably never smoke again after that."

She and Becca devised a plan and drew up a schedule so that one or both of them could keep an eye on Aunt Cecelia all day. Especially after breakfast, after lunch, and after dinner — Aunt Cecelia's favorite times to smoke.

Jessi was covering the after-breakfast shift, since it was Becca's turn to clear the table. The family had just finished a huge Saturday morning breakfast: pancakes, bacon and eggs, toast, juice, and fruit. As they sat back, satisfied and full, Jessi snuck a glance at Aunt Cecelia. She knew, just knew, that her aunt was dying for a cigarette.

Next, Jessi looked at Aunt Cecelia's Smoke-out pledge form, which was propped up in the middle of the table. There was Aunt Cecelia's signature. No question about it. Jessi saw Aunt Cecelia glance at the pledge. She saw Aunt Cecelia frown. Then she saw Aunt Cecelia push back from the table.

"Guess I'll go check on my tulips," she announced.

Jessi and Becca exchanged a glance. Neither one of them moved a muscle. Jessi waited until Aunt Cecelia left the room. Then she stretched, as casually as possible, and stood up herself. "Great pancakes, Dad," she said as she picked up her plate and glass and took them over to the sink. "Guess I'll go check on my . . . my toe shoes." She and Becca had agreed that it would probably be best if their parents didn't know about the spying they'd planned to do.

Jessi tiptoed down the hall, listening for Aunt Cecelia's footsteps. There was no sound, so Jessi figured she must already have slipped out the sliding glass doors that lead from the Ramsey dining room to the backyard. Jessi headed for those same doors.

She slid them open quietly and tiptoed out onto the deck.

"Looking for someone?"

Jessi jumped. Then she turned and saw Aunt Cecelia glaring at her.

"Don't trust your old aunt, huh?" asked Aunt Cecelia. She had one hand on her hip and the other behind her back, and she sounded angry. Jessi didn't know what to say.

Then Aunt Cecelia laughed. "I can't blame you, honey," she said. "I am just about the sneakiest smoker ever. But when I signed that pledge, I meant it."

Jessi wanted to believe Aunt Cecelia, but she was still just the tiniest bit suspicious. She took a step closer and tried to sniff without Aunt Cecelia noticing. After all, what was Aunt Cecelia hiding behind her back, if not a cigarette?

Aunt Cecelia laughed again and brought her

hand around to the front. She was holding a large bouquet of bright red tulips.

The only thing Jessi could smell was their faintly sweet scent, and the only thing she could think to say was, "Oops. Sorry." Then she hugged Aunt Cecelia.

"You know, honey," said Aunt Cecelia, "this Smokeout is such a good idea that I think I'm going to try it again tomorrow. What do you think of that?"

Jessi smiled up at her. "I think that would be excellent," she said. "Totally excellent."

Watson is full of surprises, no question about it. I knew he took this pledge seriously, but I didn't know what lengths he would go to in order to prove that . . . .

On Saturday morning, Watson showed up for breakfast wearing a tux.

"Jacket," Kristy told us later, "pants, starched white shirt, black bow tie, plaid cummerbund — or whatever you call those things — and shiny black shoes. The whole outfit."

The family was gathered around the huge kitchen table: Kristy's mom, Nannie, Charlie and Sam, David Michael, Karen, Andrew, and Emily Michelle. The room had been full of noisy talk and the clatter of dishes. When Watson showed up there was a sudden, shocked silence.

Then, after a few seconds, everybody started talking at once.

"Um, Daddy? Are you going to a wedding or something?" Karen wanted to know.

"Did we have plans I've forgotten about?" Kristy's mom asked, sounding panicked.

"Looking good, Watson," Kristy said, grinning and giving him the thumbs-up.

"Sharp threads, man," agreed Charlie, nodding.

"Can I borrow that suit for my prom?" asked Sam.

Emily Michelle just stared at Watson as if he were some stranger she'd never seen before.

Watson stood there, looking as if he were about to burst out laughing. "I want you all to finish breakfast and then run upstairs and dress in your best clothes," he said when he could fit a word in. "I'm having a little ceremony this morning, and I want you all to be there."

It was then that Kristy noticed the ornately carved wooden box Watson had tucked beneath his arm. "What's in the box?" she asked.

"Some very good companions," Watson answered. "Companions I'm going to be saying good-bye to."

That was all he'd say. He waved away their questions as he toasted and buttered a bagel. "The sooner you're all dressed, the sooner we can begin," he told them.

They finished breakfast in record time. Kristy's mom said it was okay to leave the dirty dishes on the table for once. Then everybody headed upstairs to figure out what to wear.

Kristy doesn't enjoy dressing up, which meant it wasn't hard to decide between the two fancy dresses she owns, both of which are left over from weddings. She scrambled into one of them, ran a brush through her hair, debated whether to wear pantyhose and decided not to, stuck her feet into the one pair of shoes she owns that aren't sneakers, and ran back downstairs without even checking herself in the mirror.

Watson waited until everyone was assembled in the front hall. Charlie and Sam came downstairs dressed in suits. David Michael had dressed in a polo shirt and khakis. Andrew was wearing a clean shirt and his newest jeans, and Karen had pulled on a frilly pink dress. Kristy's mom had dressed Emily Michelle in a white jumper, and herself in a full-length black gown she's worn to fancy charity dinners.

"You all look very nice," Watson said. "Thank you. And now, will you accompany me outside?" He bowed and offered his arm to his wife. Then the two of them led the others into the backyard.

Beneath one of the apple trees was a small but deep hole, surrounded by cut flowers arranged into bright bouquets. Watson asked his family to stand in a circle around the hole.

"We are gathered here today," he said solemnly, "to bid good-bye to . . ." he paused and flipped open the box, ". . . to some very dear friends."

"Watson! Your expensive cigars!" said Kristy's mom.

True enough. The box was full of cigars, each with a colorful ring. Kristy could smell their rich scent.

"That's right," said Watson. "I've been saving these for a special occasion, and I think that special occasion is now. But instead of smoking them, I'm going to put them to rest for good." He glanced wistfully at the cigars. Then he took one last sniff, smiled sadly, and closed the box. He knelt down and placed it in the hole he'd dug. Then he picked up the hose, which was lying nearby. "This is just to make sure I don't sneak out here and dig them up some night when I'm feeling weak," he explained as he held the nozzle over the box. "Charlie, would you turn on the faucet?"

So that was Kristy's Smokeout memory:

Watson in a tux, surrounded by well-dressed family members, holding a hose over a box of very valuable cigars. "I didn't even think of taking a picture," she said later, "but I guess I don't need one. I'll never forget that image."

Watch out: the Smokeout Patrol is on the road! Suppliers of carrots and gum, upholders of truth and justice, friends in need ...

Abby had a terrific time on Smokeout Day. She and a posse of kids — Buddy and Lindsey, James and Mathew and Charlotte — visited some of the people who had signed pledges. They carried pamphlets Dr. Johanssen had given them, along with snacks to ease the cravings of the quitters. They offered psychological support, encouragement, and lots of laughs to everyone they visited.

Mrs. Hobart had already been through a jumbo bag of carrots by the time they came, but she accepted several more, plus a few packs of gum. "This is harder than I thought it would be," she confessed. "But your visit really helps." She hugged everybody.

Hugging was big that day. "I never thought

133

I'd be thanking somebody for keeping me from smoking," said Mr. Spinoli when they stopped to see him at the hardware store. "But you kids have done a good thing here. It's the first time I've even tried to quit in years."

Mr. DeWitt wasn't so upbeat. In fact, he seemed more than a little cranky. But even he admitted that the Smokeout was a great idea. And he warned Lindsey and Buddy, in front of everyone, that if he ever heard about them experimenting with cigarettes again they'd be grounded until they were thirty-five years old.

By the end of that day, Kristy, Abby, and Jessi agreed that the Smokeout had to be termed a success. "We raised public awareness, we convinced a few people to try quitting for real, and lest we forget," said Kristy, "we had a great time." It looked as if the Great Stoneybrook Smokeout might become an annual event.

CHAPTER 15

Kristy, Abby, and Jessi will always remember those great moments from the day of the Smokeout. I have some memories from that Saturday, too, memories from the last night of Fashion Week. Certain moments and images will always stay with me.

For example, there's the image of the hustle and bustle of the dressing room in the last minutes before the final show was about to start. Models scurried back and forth between hair and makeup stations and the clothing racks, scrambling to be ready by the time the lights snapped on and the music started to pound.

There'd been excitement in the air before the other shows that week, but that afternoon the feeling was especially intense. It was funny, though — something was missing. I took a second to think it over, and as I did, I saw Cynthia offer to zip up the back of Harmony's dress. Cooperation. The competition was over now —

that was what was missing — and nobody had anything to gain by being nasty. Everybody suddenly had the same goal. We all wanted the final show to be a success.

We'd been through so much together that week. And I realized that, in spite of ourselves, we'd become something like friends.

Even Cokie had entered into the new spirit of cooperation. I saw her passing out bottled water she'd brought from the catering table as she flitted around, wishing everyone luck. That's an image for the scrapbook! I wished I had a camera, since I knew my friends would never believe Cokie could be so nice.

Another memory? The moment when Claudia came to find me and dragged me off to a backstage corner that looked out into the still-empty auditorium. "You have to see this to believe it," she whispered, pointing into the darkness.

It took my eyes a second or two to adjust. Then I saw what she was pointing out. The auditorium wasn't empty after all. Way in the back sat two people, arms entwined, faces attached at the lip. Sydney and Roger Bellair. Making out like crazy.

"Guess the old flame is still burning," Claudia whispered.

I had to hold in my giggles until we'd raced back to the dressing room. Then I exploded. I don't know exactly why it was so funny, but trust me — it was.

There was a more serious moment I'll remember, too, when Cynthia and I found ourselves alone together in the lounge of the women's room. She was already made up and her hair was done, but she was still wearing a smock. It was too early to put on the outfits we'd be wearing in the show.

"This has been fun," she said, smiling wistfully. "There's a lot I really love about modeling."

"But?" I prompted. I had the feeling there was more she wanted to say.

"But I've made a decision." She took a deep breath. "I'm going to quit. For awhile, anyway. Maybe forever. I don't know yet." She looked down at her hands. "All I know is that I feel as if I'm missing out on real life."

"Real life isn't always that great," I said. "You might be bored. Or worse." The image of Alan Gray — the most immature, irritating boy in eighth grade — swam into my head. What on earth would Cynthia think of boys like that? What would she think of going to school every day, and eating in the cafeteria, and going to dances where boys like Alan acted like jerks? As a model, Cynthia had been living in the fast lane with sophisticated people. She was going to be experiencing some major culture shock.

Maybe she'd hate me for steering her away from modeling. "Are you really sure?" I asked, suddenly hesitant.

"I'm sure," she said. "I know it'll be boring. I *want* boring. I crave boring!" She grinned. "And I promise not to blame you if it doesn't work out."

It was as if she'd read my mind.

"In fact," she continued, "I'll always remember how nice you were to talk to me and take me seriously. I don't think anybody's listened to me — really *listened* — in a long time." She wasn't grinning anymore. Now she looked solemn, and tears welled up in her eyes.

I hugged her. "Friends?" I asked.

"Friends," she said, hugging me back.

"Promise to keep in touch. I want to know how it all turns out."

"I will," she said. "I promise." She checked her watch. "Oh, man. I bet Mrs. Maslin is looking for us."

"You're right. We better go. But hey, Cynthia — good luck, okay?"

"Thanks. Thanks a lot."

When I entered the dressing room after talking with Cynthia, I spotted Harmony and her mom, deep in conversation. No way did I want to be involved in their argument, so I changed course and headed across the room in the opposite direction.

"Stacey!"

Oops. Too late. They'd spotted me. "Hi, Harmony," I said, pasting a smile on my face. "Hi, Mrs. Skye."

Surprisingly, Mrs. Skye smiled back.

"Stacey, Mom and I were just talking about my career plans," said Harmony.

Uh-oh. "You mean you're going to keep modeling?" I asked.

She shook her head, smiling. "No way," she answered. "We're thinking I should go into either medicine or law. What do you think?" She glanced at her mom. "Mom's finally coming around," she stage-whispered to me.

"I think you have awhile to decide," I answered. I knew that, whatever she decided to be, Harmony would probably always have her mother hovering around in the background, pushing her to do better and work harder. But maybe, as long as her career was her choice, Harmony could learn to live with that.

My next memories are a jumble of lights and music and walking down the runway and racing through the dressing room to change so I could walk again. I remember seeing my mom and my friends in the audience, and hearing them cheer and whistle and applaud. I remember Mrs. Maslin running around so fast that she was almost a blur, like a cartoon character. And I remember feeling pretty, and special, and proud. Modeling may not be my chosen career, and it's definitely not rocket science, but it sure can be fun.

I know I'm not the only one who will always remember the finale of that show. It was breathtaking. I watched it from a corner of the stage, along with most of the other models.

The music changed from a hard-driving rock beat to a romantic ballad. The lights softened and lost some of their harshness. The crowd grew quiet. And then Blaine walked onto the runway.

She wore a long gown of shimmery pink material. Her hair flowed down her back, and the tiara on her head sparkled in the lights. She walked as if she were real, live royalty instead of a pretend princess, floating along gracefully with her head held high as she smiled down at the audience.

She was absolutely radiant.

But it was Emily who stole the show. Emily Maslin, dressed as a lady-in-waiting in a smaller, simpler version of Blaine's gown, looked lovely beyond her years. I knew she was just a little kid, but I — and everyone else in the room — could suddenly see that she was going to be a beautiful young woman someday soon.

I remember glancing at Dylan Trueheart. The look on his face was unmistakable: he saw it, too. He knew she could go all the way to the top if that was what she wanted. (Later, I heard him talking to Mrs. Maslin, promising her the world if she'd only let him represent Emily. Mrs. Maslin told him she'd think about it in a few years, when Emily turned fifteen — if she still wanted to model by then.)

There's one more image I'll take with me from Fashion Week: the image of the dressing room, which had begun to feel like home, after the show was over. Clothes were draped everywhere. Makeup and hair supplies lay jumbled together on the counters. Piles of shoes and accessories filled every corner.

I glanced around the room, feeling just a tiny bit wistful about saying good-bye to the glamour, the excitement, the fun (not that I'd call almost being killed fun). But then I turned away from it, ready to head home and back to my real life.

Family, school, and the BSC — they were all I really wanted. In the past week, I'd come to value my normal, boring life more than ever, and suddenly I couldn't wait to plunge back into it.

Ann M. Martin

About the Author

ANN MATTHEWS MARTIN was born on August 12, 1955. She grew up in Princeton, NJ, with her parents and her younger sister, Jane.

Although Ann used to be a teacher and then an editor of children's books, she's now a full-time writer. She gets ideas for her books from many different places. Some are based on personal experiences. Others are based on childhood memories and feelings. Many are written about contemporary problems or events.

All of Ann's characters, even the members of the Baby-sitters Club, are made up. (So is Stoneybrook.) But many of her characters are based on real people. Sometimes Ann names her characters after people she knows, other times she chooses names she likes.

In addition to the Baby-sitters Club books, Ann Martin has written many other books for children. Her favorite is *Ten Kids, No Pets* because she loves big families and she loves animals. Her favorite Baby-sitters Club book is *Kristy's Big Day*. (By the way, Kristy is her favorite baby-sitter!)

Ann M. Martin now lives in New York with her cats, Gussie and Woody. Her hobbies are reading, sewing, and needlework — especially making clothes for children.

Look for Mystery #30

KRISTY AND THE MYSTERY TRAIN

The lights of the tunnel flashed by, a dim strobe that brightened, then plunged us into the dark over and over again. It was a sort of spooky special effect, in my opinion, but I didn't say so aloud.

Suddenly Daniel's grip tightened even more. "Do you hear someone?"

We were silent. Then I heard the sound of a voice from the other end of the car. The voice sounded angry.

"Shhh," I said. Then I said, "Daniel, Todd, stay here. *Don't move.*"

Stacey and I crept quietly forward.

The voice grew louder. "You cretin. You're early. You shouldn't be on this train. *I* should be on this train."

The other figure neither moved nor spoke.

Bright, dark, bright, the tunnel lights flashed by. The open door between the glassed-in area and the raised platform of the rear deck thumped rhythmically against the wall.

The voice continued, rising hysterically. "I'm going to tell everyone the truth, do you hear me. The truth *you* can't live with!"

The shadows made everything seem to move. Did the figure turn? Did it move away? Or did it have a chance to move before the speaker screamed. . . .

We flashed out of the tunnel and the speaker suddenly seemed to rise in the air over the railing of the open-air observation deck and plunge down, down, down.

"No," Stacey hissed. "He just pushed that guy over the rail!"

I gasped as the second man turned. Was he going to turn toward us? Catch us? Push us out of the train, too?

My knees went weak. Automatically, I pushed Daniel behind me.

The man ran forward — but along the outside walkway of the observation car.

The train whistled again.

Or was it the long, drawn-out scream of a dying man as he fell out of a train to his doom?

Read all the books
about **Stacey**
in the Baby-sitters Club series
by Ann M. Martin

Mysteries:

Portrait Collection:

Collect 'em all!

100 (and more)
Reasons to Stay Friends Forever!

More titles... ➤

The Baby-sitters Club titles continued...

❑ MG48226-2	#82	Jessi and the Troublemaker	$3.99
❑ MG48235-1	#83	Stacey vs. the BSC	$3.50
❑ MG48228-9	#84	Dawn and the School Spirit War	$3.50
❑ MG48236-X	#85	Claudi Kishi, Live from WSTO	$3.50
❑ MG48227-0	#86	Mary Anne and Camp BSC	$3.50
❑ MG48237-8	#87	Stacey and the Bad Girls	$3.50
❑ MG22872-2	#88	Farewell, Dawn	$3.50
❑ MG22873-0	#89	Kristy and the Dirty Diapers	$3.50
❑ MG22874-9	#90	Welcome to the BSC, Abby	$3.99
❑ MG22875-1	#91	Claudia and the First Thanksgiving	$3.50
❑ MG22876-5	#92	Mallory's Christmas Wish	$3.50
❑ MG22877-3	#93	Mary Anne and the Memory Garden	$3.99
❑ MG22878-1	#94	Stacey McGill, Super Sitter	$3.99
❑ MG22879-X	#95	Kristy + Bart = ?	$3.99
❑ MG22880-3	#96	Abby's Lucky Thirteen	$3.99
❑ MG22881-1	#97	Claudia and the World's Cutest Baby	$3.99
❑ MG22882-X	#98	Dawn and Too Many Sitters	$3.99
❑ MG69205-4	#99	Stacey's Broken Heart	$3.99
❑ MG69206-2	#100	Kristy's Worst Idea	$3.99
❑ MG69207-0	#101	Claudia Kishi, Middle School Dropout	$3.99
❑ MG69208-9	#102	Mary Anne and the Little Princess	$3.99
❑ MG69209-7	#103	Happy Holidays, Jessi	$3.99
❑ MG45575-3		Logan's Story Special Edition Readers' Request	$3.25
❑ MG47118-X		Logan Bruno, Boy Baby-sitter	
		Special Edition Readers' Request	$3.50
❑ MG47756-0		Shannon's Story Special Edition	$3.50
❑ MG47686-6		The Baby-sitters Club Guide to Baby-sitting	$3.25
❑ MG47314-X		The Baby-sitters Club Trivia and Puzzle Fun Book	$2.50
❑ MG48400-1		BSC Portrait Collection: Claudia's Book	$3.50
❑ MG22864-1		BSC Portrait Collection: Dawn's Book	$3.50
❑ MG69181-3		BSC Portrait Collection: Kristy's Book	$3.99
❑ MG22865-X		BSC Portrait Collection: Mary Anne's Book	$3.99
❑ MG48399-4		BSC Portrait Collection: Stacey's Book	$3.50
❑ MG92713-2		The Complete Guide to The Baby-sitters Club	$4.95
❑ MG47151-1		The Baby-sitters Club Chain Letter	$14.95
❑ MG48295-5		The Baby-sitters Club Secret Santa	$14.95
❑ MG45074-3		The Baby-sitters Club Notebook	$2.50
❑ MG44783-1		The Baby-sitters Club Postcard Book	$4.95

Available wherever you buy books...or use this order form.

Scholastic Inc., P.O. Box 7502, 2931 E. McCarty Street, Jefferson City, MO 65102

Please send me the books I have checked above. I am enclosing $_____
(please add $2.00 to cover shipping and handling). Send check or money order—
no cash or C.O.D.s please.

Name_____ Birthdate_____

Address _____

City_____ State/Zip _____

BSC5962

THE BABY-SITTERS CLUB®

by Ann M. Martin

Collect and read these exciting BSC Super Specials, Mysteries, and Super Mysteries along with your favorite Baby-sitters Club books!

More titles ➡

The Baby-sitters Club books continued...

❑ BAI47049-3	#11 Claudia and the Mystery at the Museum	$3.50
❑ BAI47050-7	#12 Dawn and the Surfer Ghost	$3.50
❑ BAI47051-5	#13 Mary Anne and the Library Mystery	$3.50
❑ BAI47052-3	#14 Stacey and the Mystery at the Mall	$3.50
❑ BAI47053-1	#15 Kristy and the Vampires	$3.50
❑ BAI47054-X	#16 Claudia and the Clue in the Photograph	$3.99
❑ BAI48232-7	#17 Dawn and the Halloween Mystery	$3.50
❑ BAI48233-5	#18 Stacey and the Mystery at the Empty House	$3.50
❑ BAI48234-3	#19 Kristy and the Missing Fortune	$3.50
❑ BAI48309-9	#20 Mary Anne and the Zoo Mystery	$3.50
❑ BAI48310-2	#21 Claudia and the Recipe for Danger	$3.50
❑ BAI22866-8	#22 Stacey and the Haunted Masquerade	$3.50
❑ BAI22867-6	#23 Abby and the Secret Society	$3.99
❑ BAI22868-4	#24 Mary Anne and the Silent Witness	$3.99
❑ BAI22869-2	#25 Kristy and the Middle School Vandal	$3.99
❑ BAI22870-6	#26 Dawn Schafer, Undercover Baby-sitter	$3.99

BSC Super Mysteries

❑ BAI48311-0	The Baby-sitters' Haunted House Super Mystery #1	$3.99
❑ BAI22871-4	Baby-sitters Beware Super Mystery #2	$3.99
❑ BAI69180-5	Baby-sitters' Fright Night Super Mystery #3	$4.50

Available wherever you buy books...or use this order form.

Scholastic Inc., P.O. Box 7502, 2931 East McCarty Street, Jefferson City, MO 65102-7502

Please send me the books I have checked above. I am enclosing $ _____
(please add $2.00 to cover shipping and handling). Send check or money order
— no cash or C.O.D.s please.

Name_____Birthdate_____

Address _____

City_____State/Zip_____

Please allow four to six weeks for delivery. Offer good in the U.S. only. Sorry, mail orders are not available to residents of Canada. Prices subject to change.

BSCM496